THE SECRET HE HOLDS

SANDI LYNN

Sandi Lynn Romance, LLC

The Secret He Holds

New York Times, USA Today & Wall Street Journal Bestselling Author
SANDI LYNN

The Secret He Holds
Copyright © 2015 Sandi Lynn

All rights reserved. No part of this publication may be reproduced, distributed, or transmitted in any form or by any means, including photocopying, recording, or other electronic or mechanical methods, without the publisher's prior written permission.
This is a work of fiction. Names, characters, places, and incidents are the products of the author's imagination or are used fictitiously. Any resemblance to actual events, locales, or persons, living or dead, is entirely coincidental.

Photographer: Wander Aguiar
Model: Lucas

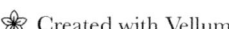 Created with Vellum

Mission Statement

Sandi Lynn Romance

Providing readers with romance novels that will whisk them away
to another world and from the daily grind of life – one book at a time.

Chapter One

As soon as we boarded the plane, I put my bag in the overhead above our first-class seats. It was heavy and overloaded with all the souvenirs and shopping we did in Vegas, or should I say that I did. Brendon, my boyfriend of six years, planned this little trip, which I thought would only be the two of us, but as usual, he invited a few of his friends to tag along—friends that I couldn't stand. Arrogant, self-absorbed, and womanizing rich boys.

"Thanks for your help." I glared at Brendon as I took my seat next to him.

"It's your shit. Not mine. You were the one who did all the shopping, so deal with it."

"You're an ass."

"And you're a bitch."

I slowly shook my head and glanced at the gentleman staring at me from across the aisle. For the love of God, he was hot. I gave him a friendly smile and then looked away. Brendon took out his iPad and began to check his emails just as the captain announced over the speakers that there was a slight delay in take-off. I sighed and reached into my purse to grab my Kindle.

"Shit."

"What?" Brendon asked.

"I thought I put my Kindle in my purse. I must have put it in my bag." I sighed as I got up and reached for the overhead.

I looked at Brendon when I was having trouble reaching my bag and taking it down.

"Can you please help me? You're a lot taller than I am."

"Fuck no. Like I said, it's your shit, not mine. Just sit your ass down and watch a movie or something. For fuck's sake, Gabby, you're driving me nuts already," he spewed as he put his beats on.

I flinched when I felt a light touch against the small of my back.

"Here. Let me help you since your friend over there won't," a rugged voice spoke.

As the hot gentleman took down my bag, I moved out of the way. "Get what you need, and I'll put it back up for you."

"Thank you." I softly smiled while the feeling of belittlement and embarrassment coursed through my veins.

I unzipped the front pocket and pulled out my Kindle. He picked up my bag and put it back in the overhead.

"Thank you again," I said quietly as I took my seat.

"Hey, man. Thanks for helping out. She does some stupid things sometimes," Brendon said.

The man didn't look at him. He looked at me and quietly spoke, "You're welcome," and then proceeded to give Brendon a dirty look.

I turned on my Kindle and flipped to a page in a book I

had started reading by the pool in Vegas. I couldn't concentrate on the words that sat on the page. The only thing on my mind was the hot guy sitting across the aisle seat. How he wore his sandy brown hair was exactly how I wished Brendon would wear his. His piercing blue eyes caught my attention the minute I looked over at him, and his perfect five-o'clock shadow graced his beautiful square jawline. His dark grey tailored suit screamed high end, with his white shirt hiding underneath and matching heather grey and black striped tie. I gulped, just thinking about him. He was easy to check out while he was reaching for my bag, but it also helped that I had a photographic memory.

After we finally took off, Brendon called for the flight attendant and asked for a bourbon. She nodded her head and then looked at me.

"Can I get you anything?"

"I'll have a glass of white wine. Whatever you have is fine."

"Sure." She smiled as she touched my shoulder.

She turned to the hot guy across the aisle and asked him. He looked over at me, and his mouth curved as he spoke. "I'll have a glass of white wine as well. Whatever you have is fine."

My heart started to beat rapidly, and I looked down at my Kindle with a smile. After the flight attendant brought us our drinks, I reached into my purse and pulled out a chocolate bar.

"Are you really going to eat that?" Brendon asked with irritation.

"Yes. Why? Would you like some?"

"What did we talk about in Vegas? Remember I showed you those hot girls in the string bikinis and told you that you could look like that, and you said you would work on it? Remember? Now you're going to blow it by eating that candy bar?"

"You're right. I'm sorry, baby," I replied nervously, putting the candy bar in my purse.

"That's more like it. You know I love you, sweets, but sometimes you just need a push in the right direction."

I looked down at my Kindle and could feel the guy from across the aisle staring at me. I was scared to look at him, and I knew I'd probably start to cry if I did. I could already feel the tears creeping up into my eyes.

Chapter Two

Brendon Sommers and I had dated for six years. We met on the first day of our freshman year at Cornell, where I graduated with an MBA in Marketing, and he graduated with an MBA in Finance and Economics. He was being groomed to take over the family's property development company. Once we graduated and Brendon's father gave him one of the penthouses he owned, he asked me to move in with him. My best friend, Giana, told me not to do it because she hated Brendon, and the two of them never got along, but I did anyway because I loved him, and I knew he loved me too, even if he acted like an ass sometimes—okay, most of the time. He was the first guy ever to love me and want to take care of me. He and Giana were the only family I had. They were the only ones who knew the real story of how I grew up. It was actually how Giana and I met. Without either of them, I'd be completely alone in the world, and Brendon reminded me of that every day.

After graduating from college, Giana took a job at a prestigious law firm in Seattle as a litigation paralegal. I missed her, and every time I'd make plans to visit, Brendon would find some way to fuck it up. I swear he did it on purpose.

I kept stealing little glances at the guy across the aisle as I pretended to read. He was on his laptop, and he looked so confident and poised. He was definitely a corporate man. His eyes diverted my way, and I quickly looked back down at my Kindle.

When we finally landed in New York, the man from across the aisle stood up, took down my bag, and handed it to me with a smile.

"I hope you enjoyed the flight."

"I did. Thank you." I smiled back as I took the bag from him.

"Tell your friend there that I said he's a complete dick, and you can do better than him."

He held out his hand and motioned for me to exit the plane first while he followed, leaving Brendon at least two people behind me.

"What the fuck? Did you see what that guy did? He let you out and cut me off. I should have decked him."

"Let it go, Brendon. We're both tired, and you need a good night's sleep. God knows you haven't gotten any in the last four days."

"It was all worth it, sweets."

As we exited the airport doors, I watched the man sitting across the aisle from me on the plane climb into a black limousine and pull away.

～

"I want to hear all about your weekend in Vegas!" Giana exclaimed over Facetime.

"It was okay."

"Okay? That's it? It's Vegas, Gabby. How could it be just okay?"

"It's hard to have a good time when your boyfriend forgets that you're with him and takes off with his friends, claiming he thought I was behind him. It was one big drunkfest, G. The bromance exploded in Vegas."

"I bet they all fucked each other too."

I laughed.

"I'm being serious, Gabby. I wouldn't put it past those dickwads to line up and have one big orgy with each other."

"Oh my God. You have to stop." I laughed uncontrollably.

"So, did you do anything exciting?"

"I shopped and gambled a bit."

"Did you win?"

"Three thousand dollars," I said as I held up the wad of cash.

"Way to go! I hope you didn't tell No Balls that."

"No, I didn't. I'll just discreetly deposit it into my savings account."

"Good girl."

"Can I tell you something?"

"Sure, Gabs. What's up?"

"I sort of met this guy on the plane coming back to New York, and I can't stop thinking about him."

"Oh?" she said as she pressed her face up against the screen. I hated it when she did that.

"He was beautiful, G. So damn beautiful."

"Hold up," she said as she put up her hand. "Who says that a guy is beautiful?"

"Okay, fine. He was sexy as fuck, and he wore a really expensive suit. He helped me with my bag because Brendon wouldn't get out of his seat."

"He sounds dreamy. Was he old?"

"He looked to be in his early thirties."

"Tall, short, white, black? I need more details." She smiled.

"He was about six feet one. Maybe six two."

"Skinny, fat, muscular?"

"From what I could see, he had a nice body. He was wearing a suit, so I really couldn't tell. But the point is, I can't stop thinking about him. He really got to me."

"Listen, Gabby, and please don't be offended when I tell you this. He was a sweet man who helped you. Of course, you're going to fall for him. You're living with someone who pretends to be a real man. A person who doesn't give a shit about you. I'm sorry. You're twenty-four years old. You should be out having fun. Not stuck at home waiting on that spineless piece of shit twenty-four-seven."

I sighed. "Brendon loves me, and I am having fun."

"How many times did you have sex in Vegas?" she asked. "Why are you hesitating to answer my question? You did have sex, right?"

"No," I replied as I looked away from the computer.

"WHAT! WHO GOES TO VEGAS WITH THEIR BOYFRIEND AND DOESN'T HAVE SEX?!" she yelled with her hands flying around.

"He was drunk most of the time or out all night with his friends."

"While you sat in the hotel room by yourself?" she asked with a frown. "Wake up, Gabby. I can't stand to see you being treated like that anymore. For fuck's sake. I know damn well he had sex with other women in Vegas or at least with his boy toys."

"He would never cheat on me."

"UGH, Gabby!" she exclaimed.

"I have to go, G. I need to figure out what to make for dinner before Brendon gets home."

"Well, whatever you make, I hope he chokes on it."

I rolled my eyes. "I'll talk to you later."

I got up from my chair and took some chicken from the freezer. I scoured my produce drawer and had enough vegetables to make a stir-fry.

It was around eight o'clock when Brendon walked through the door.

"Hey," he said as he walked over and kissed my cheek.

"You smell like a woman." My brows furrowed.

"You just wouldn't believe the day I had. We hired this new secretary, and I swear she bathed in her perfume before coming to the office. I had to tell her that she can't wear it anymore, or else I'd have to let her go."

"It was that bad?"

"Yeah, babe. It was that bad. Everything she handed me reeked of her perfume. I'm actually going to take a quick shower to wash it off. It's making me sick."

I smiled as I began unbuttoning his shirt. "I can help you wash it all off."

He took hold of my hands and put them down. "Sorry, babe. If I let you do that, we won't eat until later, and I'm starving. Give me ten minutes. It smells amazing in here. I can't wait to eat." He winked as he headed to the bathroom.

As I was getting ready for bed, I caught Brendon staring at me through the full-length mirror.

"Thank you for dinner. It was good. I like coming home after a long work day to your home-cooked meals."

He walked over and placed his hands on my hips as his lips trailed across my neck.

"You're welcome."

"I know it's been a while since we fucked, but if you're up to it, I'm game. But first, let me turn off the light."

"Why can't we have sex with the lights on for once?" I asked.

He pushed a strand of my hair behind my ear. "You know why. You still have some toning up to do. We've talked about this."

He led me over to the bed, and we made love the same way we'd done for the past six years: missionary style and with the lights off. He laid me down and crammed it in. There was no foreplay involved unless he had trouble getting hard. Then he told me to stroke him. As I rolled over and lay on my side of the bed, I couldn't help feeling depressed. It was the same feeling I got every time we made love. There was no satisfaction in it for me except the emotional aspect of him wanting me. If he didn't love me, then he wouldn't want to have sex with me.

Tomorrow after work, I was going to hit the gym hard.

Chapter Three

THREE MONTHS LATER

I worked a daily job of nine to five at Holster Marketing Firm, which handled the account of a major upscale retailer. When I walked in, my boss, Kendra, called me into her office.

"Sit down, Gabby."

The way she said it didn't sound good. She took off her glasses and folded her hands on her desk.

"As you've been aware, the account you're handling has been going under for quite a while. It's not your fault or the fault of anyone in this firm. It's the retailer's poor management and decision-making that dragged them down. Anyway, they filed for bankruptcy and are closing fifty of their stores around the country. When they cut, we have to cut."

"Are you firing me?" I asked in shock.

"Not firing. Laying off. We can't afford to keep you and your team anymore since we're losing the account."

"But I worked my ass off on that account," I said as tears sprang to my eyes.

"I know, and believe me, you're one of our best, but we have to go by the numbers. Unfortunately, we have to lay off at least five people today. I'm so sorry. You're a smart and bright woman. You'll find something else, and I'll give you the best recommendation. This is New York. There are tons of marketing jobs out there."

I sat there in disbelief and shook my head. I couldn't believe this was happening.

"I understand. Thank you, Kendra."

As I got up from the chair, she walked over and gave me a light hug. "You never know. This may be the best thing that ever happened to you."

I gave her a small smile as I walked out of her office and back to my cubicle. A box was already sitting on my desk for me to start packing my things. I pulled my phone from my purse and dialed Brendon. It went straight to voicemail, so I called Giana.

"Hey, Gabby."

"I just got laid off," I said, deadpan.

"What? Are you serious?"

"They laid off five of us today."

"Listen, I'm just walking into the courtroom with Brian, so go home, take a long, hot bath, and I'll call you as soon as I get out."

"Okay. I'll talk to you later."

I cleaned out my desk and tried to call Brendon one last time before I headed home. Still no answer. This really sucked. I couldn't believe that I no longer had a job. My self-esteem fell even lower than it already was. I finally hailed a cab and set my box down next to me.

"You get canned, lady?" the cab driver so graciously asked.

"Laid off."

"Sorry to hear that."

"Thanks," I replied with a sullen look.

I paid the driver his fare and grabbed my box. As soon as I opened the door to the penthouse, I set the box down in the foyer, walked to the kitchen, and poured a glass of wine. Wine and a hot bath were what I needed right now. As I walked up the stairs and down the hallway, I stopped the second I heard noises coming from the bedroom. My heart started to pound viciously, and a rush of nerves made their way throughout my entire body. I cautiously and quietly approached the door and placed my hand over my mouth as I stood there and watched Brendon fucking some girl from behind. I listened to sounds come from him that I'd never heard before. I threw my glass of wine at the wall that the bed sat on, and instantly, Brendon turned around and put up his hands.

"Gabby, I thought you were at work."

The stench of the perfume that I once smelled on him lingered in the air. The girl, sitting on my bed, naked, asked, "Who's she?"

"I'm his girlfriend," I whispered as the tears fell down my face.

"You said you weren't seeing anyone, Brendon," she snapped as she gathered her clothes.

She walked past me and lightly touched my arm, holding her clothes tightly in a ball against her.

"I'm sorry. I didn't know." She walked out of the room.

As I stared at him, standing there, completely naked, all I could see was the way he was fucking her. A way he would never do with me.

"Gabby, baby. I can explain."

I cocked my head and looked at him like some psychotic patient that didn't understand. I walked into the bathroom and grabbed the scissors from the drawer. When

I walked back into the bedroom, I saw the fear in Brendon's eyes.

"What are you doing with those?" he said as he backed away and covered his cock with his hands.

Suddenly, it hit me. He thought I was going to cut off his dick. I burst into loud laughter as I went into the closet and cut off the airport tags on my suitcase.

"Baby, I'm sorry. I don't know why I did it. It'll never happen again," he pleaded as he placed his hand on my shoulder.

I quickly turned around and stuck the scissors up to his crotch. He froze, and his eyes widened.

"You're right. It never will happen again because we are no longer together. And if one word comes out of that filthy, disgusting mouth of yours, I will cut it off. You've belittled and humiliated me for the last time, Brendon Sommers. Do you understand me?" He slowly nodded his head. "Now, please leave this room and leave me ALONE!" I screamed in his face.

He slowly backed up, and when he was out of harm's way, he picked up his clothes from the floor and ran out of the bedroom. I locked the door so he couldn't get back in. All I wanted to do was crawl into bed and hide under the sheets. But I knew I wouldn't get out if I did, and I needed to leave this penthouse and him as soon as possible.

I stripped out of my work clothes and looked at myself in the mirror. Maybe I didn't work out hard enough. Maybe I should have gone to the gym more. My five-foot-six height and one-hundred-twenty-pound body wasn't enough for him. I moved my hand up and down my left arm. The urge was there. My fingers deftly traced the scar on my forearm where I slipped and cut too deep. Just this once and never again. I had to make the emotional pain stop. No. I promised myself I'd never go back there. I threw some clothes in the suitcase, grabbed my laptop bag, and walked down the stairs. When I reached the foyer, Brendon came running in.

"Gabby, please. Can we talk about this first? You just can't leave like this."

The anger that brewed inside me became stronger, and finally, I had a voice.

"You just can't fuck other women like that. You make me sick, Brendan Sommers. You have stabbed me in the heart a thousand times over with your actions and your words. You've embarrassed me, belittled me, and made sure that you broke down my self-esteem so low that I would have to spend the rest of my life trying to raise it back up. Giana was right. You never loved me."

"Giana's a bitch."

I couldn't believe he said that. I put my hand in front of him to stop his filthy mouth from speaking. He never took responsibility for anything he did wrong in his life.

"Go fuck yourself, Brendon. I bet you'd be really good at it." I grabbed the handle of my suitcase and rolled it behind me as I walked out the door. He followed me to the elevator.

"Have a nice life, Gabby. Don't think you'll ever meet someone who will love you because nobody could love someone like you. You're right. I never did love you. You're a game, Gabby—a pawn in someone's hand. Poor little Gabby grew up with no one to love her, and twenty-four years later, she still doesn't have anyone. Good riddance, bitch," he said as he turned and walked away.

He numbed me with his words. My legs shook so badly that I stepped in and sat down against the wall as soon as the elevator doors opened. When I reached the lobby and the doors opened, Silas, the doorman, ran over and helped me up.

"Miss McCarthy, are you okay?"

"I'm fine, Silas," I whispered as I looked straight ahead at the front doors.

"Are you going on another trip?"

"Yeah, but this time, I'm not coming back."

"Good for you, Miss McCarthy. I never liked Mr. Sommers. He was always mean to you."

I looked over at Silas and gave him a small smile. "He was, wasn't he?"

"Yes, he was. Let me get you a cab." He stepped outside the doors and whistled for a cab.

When one finally stopped, Silas loaded my bags into the trunk and gave me a hug goodbye.

～

As soon as I arrived at the airport, I walked up to the ticket counter.

"How can I help you?" the annoying, cheery girl asked.

"I need a ticket on the next flight to Seattle, please."

"Round trip?" she asked with a wide smile.

"No. One way."

"You're just in time. The next flight leaves in approximately one hour."

"Great."

After checking my luggage and clearing security, I walked to my gate and took a seat. I pulled my phone from my pocket to call Giana; it was dead, and I had left my charger at the penthouse. I started to panic because Giana's address was in my phone, and with it being dead, I had no way of pulling it up. I unzipped the inside pocket in my purse and was relieved when I found the address label I had saved from one of the packages she had sent me. I looked at the time on the wall and thought I had just enough minutes to find a shop selling phone chargers. They began boarding the plane just as I got up from my seat. I sat in my window seat and stared as we took off down the runway. As the plane lifted off the ground, I said goodbye to my old life and to New York.

Chapter Four

I arrived in Seattle at ten o'clock, hailed a cab, and was at Giana's apartment at ten fifty. I took the elevator up to the fourth floor and found apartment 4C. As I softly knocked on the door, I began to cry. I promised myself to hold it together until I got here. I guess I couldn't wait any longer.

"Who is it?" she asked.

"Giana, it's Gabby."

Within a split second, the door flew open, and her jaw dropped. She looked at me and cupped my face in her hands.

"Gabby, what are you doing here? Oh my God. Are you okay?"

The only thing I could do was shake my head no.

"Get in here," she uttered as she grabbed my laptop bag.

I wheeled in my suitcase, and before she could shut the door, I fell into her arms and sobbed like a baby.

"Shh. It's going to be all right." She softly stroked my hair.

The Secret He Holds

She led me over to the couch and tried to calm me down. "Gabby, look at me. You need to tell me what happened, sweetie."

"I walked in on Brendon and some girl fucking in our bed. Our bed!" I wailed.

"It's okay. You're better off without him. I'm so proud of you for finally leaving that dickwad. You look exhausted."

"I am, and I'm sorry for just showing up like this. I meant to call you, but my phone is dead, and I left my charger in New York."

"Don't be sorry. I'm so happy to see you. Come on. I'll show you the guest room, and you can get some sleep. We'll talk all about it in the morning."

I nodded my head as she led me to the bedroom.

"You have your own bathroom right here," she said as she turned on the bathroom light. "There's plenty of towels and washcloths in there. Go wash your face, and I'll get your nightshirt out."

I lifted my shirt over my head and walked into the bathroom. After washing my face and examining my swollen red eyes in the mirror, Giana walked in and handed me my nightshirt.

"Let me see your arms."

"I didn't. The urge was there, but I fought it."

She carefully looked them over and gave me a hug. "I'm so proud of you."

Giana pulled the covers back, and I climbed into bed. She tucked me in just like when we were kids.

"Get some sleep, ladybug." She smiled. "I'll make us breakfast in the morning, and we'll talk and figure things out when you have a clear head."

"Thank you, G."

"If you need anything, I'll be right down the hall."

She walked out of the room and only closed the door halfway. I lay there, exhausted, as I closed my eyes, and the only thing I could see was him and her.

~

I opened my eyes and took a moment to remember where I was. Yesterday seemed like such a blur, and I was hoping it was a dream, but it wasn't. The aroma of blueberry pancakes lingered throughout the apartment. I only climbed out of bed because I had to use the bathroom. I stopped and looked at myself in the mirror. My eyes were swollen and tired, and my skin looked haggard. I softly ran the brush through my hair before following the pancake smell to the kitchen.

"Good morning, sunshine." Giana smiled.

"Really?"

"I'm just trying to cheer you up." She took a mug from the cabinet and filled it with coffee. "Here. Drink up."

"Thanks."

"So this is the plan," she spoke as she set down a plate with two blueberry pancakes on it in front of me. "You're here, and you're staying. You're going to move in with me and find a job. It's time to create a new life, Gabby—a life of your own. And don't worry about paying for anything just yet. We'll discuss that after you find a job."

"I can't move in here."

"Yes, you can, and you will. It's been way too long since we've seen each other, and now that I have you here, you're not leaving. Besides, where would you go? Seattle will do you good. I promise." She smiled. "Now eat up."

I cut off a small piece of the pancake. My stomach was a wreck, and the last thing I wanted to do was eat.

"Don't you have to go to work?"

"I called in. I wanted to spend the day with you and make sure you're okay."

"I'm fine. Please go to work."

I heard the front door open, and I looked at Giana. "Are you expecting someone?"

She smiled as a tall and ruggedly handsome-looking man walked into the kitchen.

"Good morning, darling." He kissed her cheek and then turned and looked at me. "And you must be Gabby." He smiled as he held out his hand.

"And you must be?"

"Donovan Holms."

I lightly shook his hand and looked over at Giana as she poured him a cup of coffee.

"Donovan and I work together." She smiled.

"Do your coworkers just randomly show up at your apartment so early in the morning?"

"Only the hot and sexy ones." She grinned as she kissed his cheek.

I sat there confused because she had never mentioned anyone named Donovan before. I took one bite of my pancakes and pushed the plate away.

"Listen. The gala for the American Cancer Society is tonight, and you're going."

"G, no. I don't want to go anywhere. I'm not up to it."

"Yes, you are, and I don't want to hear another word about it. I'll make you a deal. If you go tonight, then I promise I won't make you do anything else. If you want to stay locked up here for the next month, I won't object."

"I don't have a dress," I said.

"I have a closet full of dresses for you to choose from. Some still have the tags on them. I know you're hurting really bad right now, but you have to pick yourself up and move on. At least for tonight."

I sighed. "I'd be a third wheel."

Donovan looked at me and smiled. "Giana and I aren't going together to the gala. So, you wouldn't be the third wheel. But you two would be the most beautiful women there."

I looked down in embarrassment. I was far from beautiful, and nobody could tell me otherwise.

"I have to go to the office, darling. I'll see you later tonight." He winked.

As I sat there sipping my coffee, I watched her blue eyes dance as he walked away.

"Were you ever going to tell me about him?" I asked.

"Eventually. I needed to see where it was going first. I think I'm falling in love with him." She smiled brightly.

"Do you think mixing work and pleasure is a good idea?"

"I don't know. I guess we'll find out."

"Is he a lawyer? How old is he?"

"Yes, he is a lawyer, and he's thirty-five. There's only one problem." She pouted.

"What's that?" I cocked my head.

"He's married."

I spit out my coffee. "What?! Giana!"

"This is why I didn't tell you about him to begin with. He said his marriage had been over for almost a year. He and his wife don't have sex, and she's a bitch."

"If their marriage is over, then why hasn't he divorced her?"

"He's going to. He said he just needs more time to get things in order. Money, properties, etc."

I slowly shook my head. "I don't trust guys like that. I think he's stringing you along."

"Your problem is that you *do* trust guys like that. Look

at Dickwad. It only took you six years to leave his sorry ass. What did he say when you left?"

I got up from the table, cleaned off my plate, and put it in the dishwasher. "He told me he never loved me." I placed my hands on the sink and paused. "I don't want to talk about him anymore. I need to go lie down for a while."

"I'm flying to New York and chopping off his balls. How dare he?"

I managed a small smile and went back to my bedroom, climbed into bed, and slept for another two hours.

"Get up, sleepyhead. We have salon appointments!" Giana exclaimed as she sat on the edge of the bed.

I rolled over and pushed her away. "No salon appointments."

"Yes." She pulled at my arm until I sat up. "You're getting out of this bed, and we're going to get pampered for tonight's gala. There are going to be very rich and influential people there. Maybe you'll meet someone."

"I don't care who's going to be there, and I'm not meeting anyone. I'm done with guys. I hate all men. Especially men with money."

"Fair enough, but we still have to get ready and go. Our appointment is in an hour, and traffic can be a bitch around here."

"Fine," I huffed. "Just remember that, after today, you can't make me do anything else."

"I won't. I made a promise, and I always keep my promises." She smiled. "Now, get up and follow me to my closet. We need to find you a dress to wear."

I stood in front of the mirror and stared at myself. My long, brown, drab hair was now the prisoner of an ombre color, going from dark to honey-toned ends that sat in an updo with cascading curls. I wore a red, embellished strap blouson dress with matching red heels. I wanted to wear the black one, but Giana told me that I was depressing enough, and I wasn't going to magnify it by wearing black. I pulled the derma blend makeup from my bag and carefully covered the scar on my arm. It was something that I was very self-conscious of and covered up when I wasn't wearing long sleeves. Giana walked into the bedroom and did a little twirl in front of me.

"How do I look?"

"Amazing and gorgeous," I replied.

Her five foot ten and size four body looked amazing in everything she put on. Her long, blonde, subtly highlighted hair lay in perfect curls along her shoulders, which complemented the soft grey shimmery short dress that hugged her body.

"Thanks, but the person who looks amazing and gorgeous is you. Tonight's the night of the start of your new life. Aren't you the least bit excited?" she asked in excitement as she took hold of my hands.

"Not really," I said as I pulled a tube of lipstick from my purse.

"No!" Giana grabbed the lipstick from my hands. "You need red lips. Not this—" she turned the tube upside down. "Berry Around Town color. I have the perfect color."

Suddenly, there was a knock at her door. I looked at her, and she bit down on her bottom lip.

"That would be Jared."

"Who's Jared, and why is he here?"

The Secret He Holds

I had a bad feeling about this.

"He's a coworker of mine, and he's escorting us to the gala. He's gay, so don't worry about it. He's my cover for Donovan tonight. Did I mention that he's bringing his wife?"

My mouth dropped, and I shook my head.

"Go let Jared in while I get your lipstick." She flitted out of the room, and I followed, walking to the door, and answering it against my will.

"Hi. You must be Gabby." He smiled.

"And you must be Jared. Come on in. G will be out in a minute." I walked to the kitchen. He followed.

"It's really good to meet you finally. Giana talks about you all the time."

"Thanks. It's good to meet you, too. Please forgive me if I come off as a bitch," I sighed. "I don't want to go to this thing, and Giana is forcing me to."

"If it makes you feel any better, I don't want to go either. I'm doing it for G and Donovan."

"You know about the two of them?"

"Yeah." He smirked. "I'm the only one at the firm who knows, and they are the only ones who know I'm gay. Word around the firm is that G and I are seeing each other. It's sort of a win-win for both of us. People think I'm straight, and they don't suspect her of dating a married man."

"That's nice of you. But I don't agree with what she and Donovan are doing."

"I don't either."

"You two need to shush," Giana said as she strolled into the kitchen.

She handed me a tube of red lipstick, and we took a cab to the gala.

Chapter Five

As I stepped through the large glass doors and into the lobby of the hotel, I gasped at its beauty. The rich colors of beige and gold gave the most elegant look. The marble floors shined brightly, as did the multiple oversized chandeliers that hung throughout. Victorian furniture filled the space with such elegance that I felt like I was transported back in time.

"I believe the gala is this way." Giana hooked her arm around Jared and gracefully strutted her way through the lobby and into the grand ballroom.

Everyone in attendance was filthy rich. You could smell money lingering in the air. I needed a drink if I was going to get through this night. I tapped Jared on the shoulder and told him I was going to the bar.

"Okay. I'll meet you over there in a few minutes. Giana wants us to move around the room so people can get a good look at us, especially Donovan's wife."

I rolled my eyes and headed to the bar.

"What may I get for you?" the sexy Italian bartender asked.

"Whiskey sour, please. Double whiskey."

"Coming right up." The corners of his mouth curved up as he pulled a glass down.

I looked around the room at all the men dressed in black and white tuxedos and the women on their arms who spent hours and probably thousands of dollars looking like the elegant wife. I couldn't help but think about how many of these men were unfaithful and how their unsuspecting wives had no clue. That's what rich men did. They play the part of the happy, loving husband, giving their wives anything they want to distract them from the multiple affairs they are having. I always knew that was what Brandon did. The girl I caught him with wasn't the first. He came home countless nights reeking of women's perfume and the lame excuse as to why. I was in denial, and I didn't want to believe that he would cheat on me. I spent my whole life looking for love, and when I thought I finally found it, I wasn't going to give up so easily. Brandon didn't just cheat; he was a manipulator and an abuser. Not physical, but emotional. He used the way I grew up to strip me of any self-confidence and dignity I had.

"Here you go, pretty lady. One whiskey sour." The bartender handed me my drink with a wide grin.

"Double the whiskey, right?" I asked.

"Of course." He grinned and moved on to the next guest.

I took my drink and walked across to where Jared and Giana were talking to Donovan and his wife. *Bold move, G.*

"Gabby, there you are. I would like you to meet Donovan Holmes and his wife, Sylvia."

With a watchful look, Donovan carefully studied my reaction to ensure I didn't slip.

"It's nice to meet you, Mr. and Mrs. Holms."

"Nice to meet you as well," Donovan replied as he lightly shook my hand.

I sipped on my whiskey sour and grabbed some bruschetta from the tray as the waiter walked by. While Giana was chatting it up with McCheater and his wife, and Jared went to the restroom, I walked over to the other side of the ballroom to check out the eight-foot-long dessert table that was set up.

"There you are. I was looking for you."

As I turned around to speak to Jared, my eyes latched on to the piercing blue eyes that caught my attention three months ago.

"What the—" I whispered as I stared at him from across the room, and his mesmerizing eyes stared back. The corners of his mouth slightly curved up into a captivating smile that sent shivers in all the right places.

My heart picked up the pace as he started to walk towards me across the crowded room. His eyes never left mine. That was until some man stopped him, whispered in his ear, and he turned around and walked out of the ballroom.

"Are you okay?" Jared asked.

"That guy," I said as I stared at the doorway.

"What guy?"

"The one who just left the room. He sat across the aisle from me on a plane about three months ago. He helped me with my bag."

"Who is he?" Jared asked.

"I don't know. We didn't exchange names."

"I'm sure he'll be back soon. When you see him, go talk to him."

As Jared and I walked to the bar, we watched Giana enter the lobby. I saw Donovan whisper in his wife's ear a few moments later. She nodded her head, smiled, and then he walked out. I was almost sure the two of them were going to have sex somewhere in this hotel. I heard my phone ding, and there was a text message from G.

"Whenever you want to leave, you can go. I'm spending the night at the hotel tonight. See you in the morning. Have fun and do yourself a favor. Meet a really hot guy. There's plenty of them here."

While Jared mingled with some of the guests he was acquainted with, I spent the next hour standing by the bar and watching for the guy from the plane to walk back into the room. He didn't. I had had enough and was more than ready to return to the apartment.

I found Jared and told him that I was leaving and that he could stay if he wanted to. He seemed to be having a good time, and he said he was going to stay back for a while longer. I had to use the restroom, so I stopped at the lobby desk and asked where the closest one was. When I was finished and made my way back to the lobby to leave, my heart stopped when I saw *him* walking towards the lobby doors, and he wasn't alone. On his arm was a beautiful blonde woman in a long, black, shimmery gown that clung to her body. *Fuck, he's married!* Shaking my head and ready to explode, I waited until they left the hotel before I went home. When I knew it was safe, I walked out the doors and told the valet that I needed a cab. As I turned around to wait, there he was, staring at me as his wife was getting into a black limo. A few seconds had passed, and a cab pulled up. Before I knew it, the door opened, and I felt a hand on the small of my back. I turned around, and he was within inches of me.

"I would like to know your name?" he asked in that sexy voice that I had longed to hear again.

At that point, I was reeling with anger. Anger that he was behaving the way he was with his wife sitting in the limo behind my cab. *Who the fuck does this guy think he is?* I looked straight into his smoldering blue eyes.

"It's none of your business." I climbed into the cab, grabbed the handle, and shut the door, pushing down on the lock from the inside. After what I said, I couldn't bring myself to look at him as the driver pulled away.

When I got back to the apartment, I took off the killer heels I was wearing and decided to take a hot bath. As I ran the water, I poured in a capful of vanilla-scented bubble bath. Stripping out of my dress, I climbed into the tub and sighed as I sank down into the hot, bubbly water. My brain was on overload and trying to process too much too soon. First with Brendon. Then with Giana and Donovan, and now the hot guy from the plane. It didn't matter anyway. I was sure he was in town for the gala, and I'd never see him again. At least I hoped that I'd never see him again.

I looked at the razor that sat on the edge of the tub as the feeling of hopelessness coursed through my veins. I picked it up and held it in my hand as the flashbacks started. Just this once. I'd been through so much lately, and seeing the man I'd thought about since the day I laid eyes on him three months ago with his wife was too much. I looked at my scar. The one thing that would always be a constant reminder. I threw the razor across the bathroom, and it landed behind the toilet. As I stepped out and dried off, I put on my pajamas and climbed into bed. I couldn't think anymore. My brain hurt, my heart hurt, and my feelings hurt. I just wanted to go to sleep and forget everything and everyone.

Chapter Six

The morning sun was shining brightly through the entryway as I walked through the living room and into the kitchen to make a pot of coffee. My head was throbbing, compliments of one too many whiskey sours last night. As I waited for the coffee to brew, I found a bottle of aspirin and chased down two white pills with a glass of water. With my phone in hand, I took my cup of coffee over to the couch and sat down to check some emails. I was surprised when I opened up the email from Kendra.

Hi, Gabby,

I just wanted to let you know that I have a friend who works for Young International, and they have an opening in their marketing department for an associate. If you don't know, Young International is one of the largest luxury hotel chains in the world. Their headquarters is based in Seattle. I don't know if you're willing to move or not, but I can call my friend and set up an interview for you. I feel really bad about having to let you go. You were one of our best employees. If you're interested, call me.

Sincerely,

Kendra Howe

I couldn't believe it as I kept reading her email over and over again. I opened up my contacts on my phone and dialed her immediately.

"This is Kendra."

"Hi, Kendra, it's Gabby. I just read your email."

"Gabby, it's good to hear from you. I don't know if you're interested in relocating or not."

"Kendra, I moved to Seattle a few days ago. I'm staying with my best friend, Giana."

"What? You moved? What about Brendon?"

"I broke up with him the day you laid me off. I came home, and he was screwing some chick from his office."

"Oh my God, Gabby. I'm so sorry. I had no idea. So you packed up and moved to Seattle?"

"Yeah. I need a fresh start with fresh people."

"Perfect. You haven't found a job yet, have you?"

"No. To be honest, I haven't started looking yet."

"Great. Let me call Peter. He's a good friend of mine, and we got to talking yesterday. He said that they were looking for someone to fill one of their vacant positions. I did tell him about you, and he sounded very interested. I'll put him in touch with you."

"Thank you, Kendra. You have no idea how much this means to me."

"Don't mention it, Gabby. It's the least I can do."

As soon as we hung up, I heard the door open, and G strolled into the living room with a smile on her face.

"It's official. I'm in love with him," she said as she plopped herself down next to me.

"So, how does it feel to be in love with a married man?" I spewed.

"Ugh, Gabby. Just because he wears a ring doesn't

mean he's married. Wait. That didn't come out right. Well, you know what I mean."

"Just be careful, G. I don't want you getting hurt."

"Don't worry about me." She smiled. "Did you have fun last night?"

"It was okay." There was no use telling her about my encounter with Airplane Guy.

"Listen, I'm sorry that I dragged you there."

"Just forget about it. I have some news."

I told her about my phone call with Kendra, and she became excited.

"See, I told you things would start looking up, and they are."

My phone began to ring in my hand. It was from an unknown number. I suspected it was Peter, so I answered it.

"Hello."

"Hi. Is this Gabrielle McCarthy?" a man asked.

"Yes. This is she."

"Hi, Gabrielle, this is Peter Landry. Our mutual friend, Kendra, forwarded me your number. She tells me you just moved to Seattle."

"Yes. I did. A few days ago."

"Well, first of all, welcome. Second of all, I would like you to come in for an interview if you're interested."

"I'm very interested. Thank you, Peter."

"No problem. I'm going to email you an application. I just need you to fill it out and email it back to me before the interview."

"Sure."

"Are you available tomorrow morning at ten o'clock?"

"Yes. Tomorrow morning will be fine," I said as I gave G a thumbs-up.

"Great. I'll see you then. I'll include the address of our building in the email I'm sending you."

"Thank you, Peter. I'll see you tomorrow."

"Bye, Gabrielle."

I hit the end button, and G reached over and gave me a hug. "Things are already moving in your favor, sweetie. I'm so happy for you."

"Don't get too excited. I don't have the job yet."

"Positivity is the key. Stay positive. The job is yours. Who could resist you?" She pouted while her fingers deftly played with the ends of my hair.

"Umm...Brendon?"

She rolled her eyes. "Dickwad doesn't count. He wouldn't know a good woman if she properly sucked his cock."

"G!" I exclaimed and then began to laugh.

"What? It's the truth. I'm going to take a shower, and then we're going shopping."

"We are?" I asked in confusion.

"Yes. You need a new outfit for your interview tomorrow. So get off your ass and get ready. On our way to the store, I'll tell you all about my magical night with Donovan."

Gee. I could hardly wait.

Chapter Seven

I stepped into the building of Young International and took the glass elevator that sat in the middle of the lobby up to the sixteenth floor. The interior of the building was magnificent and almost had the same style of décor as the hotel that held the gala. I was a nervous wreck and worried about if I looked okay. The black crew neck and sleeveless dress I was wearing hugged my curves and sat an inch above my knee. It was paired with the perfect black pointy-toe and four-inch stiletto heels. Giana called it my power outfit. As I stepped off the elevator, the redhead behind the curved desk asked if she could help me.

"I have an interview with Peter Landry."

"Ah, yes. You must be Miss McCarthy. Have a seat over there, and I'll let him know you're here."

I politely smiled and took a seat in one of the many plush chairs that sat against the wall. A few moments later, a man in a navy blue tailored suit approached me.

"Gabrielle McCarthy?" He smiled.

I stood up and lightly shook his hand.

"I'm Peter. It's nice to meet you."

"It's nice to meet you as well," I replied nervously.

"Follow me, and we'll go to my office."

He led me down the long hallway and around the corner. When we reached his office, he told me to take a seat and shut the door. Once he made himself comfortable, he offered me something to drink, and when I declined, he began the interview process.

Peter was a handsome man. I'd say he was in his early forties with salt and pepper hair that complemented his deep blue eyes.

"Why Seattle?" he asked.

"Excuse me?"

"Why did you move to Seattle?"

I sat there, poised, with my head held high. I needed this job, and I wasn't about to fall apart and tell him that I moved here because of Brendon.

"Well, it was time for a change. There was nothing more for me in New York City since Kendra laid me off, and my best friend lives here, so I thought, 'Why not?'." I smiled—a smile so fake that I prayed he wouldn't see right through me.

Suddenly, there was a knock on his office door. Without warning, it opened. My heart started racing, and I gasped when I turned around and saw him standing there. "Him" being the hot guy from the plane.

"Simon, I would like you to meet Gabrielle McCarthy. I'm interviewing her for the marketing associate position."

He held out his hand, and with the corners of his perfectly shaped lips curved upward, he spoke in a low and modulated voice. "It's a pleasure to meet you finally, Gabrielle."

I nervously extended my hand until it was in the palm of his. An overwhelming feeling came over me when we touched; electricity sent thousands of lightning bolts throughout my body. There was something about the way he said my name that sent chills down my spine.

"I'm Simon Young, CEO of this fine company you're interviewing for."

I swallowed hard, and the only words that could escape my lips were, "Nice to meet you."

He walked over to Peter's desk and picked up my resume. "I can take over from here, Peter. I'll let you know when we're done."

Peter looked at him strangely as he got up from his chair. "Okay. I'll be down the hall."

Simon took a seat in Peter's chair and leaned back, studying my resume. He looked up from the white paper he was holding and then studied me. He looked just as sexy as the first time I saw him on the airplane and the second time I saw him at the gala. I felt uncomfortable as his eyes stared into mine. I looked down.

"So, you want to work for my company, and you want to move to Seattle?"

"I—"

"There's no need to be nervous, Gabrielle. Regardless of what you may have heard about me, I don't bite—at least not hard." He winked.

I tightened my crossed legs because the sensation below was getting out of control. I needed to pull it together and stay focused on getting this job. I took in a deep breath.

"First of all, I moved here a few days ago, and I'm sorry, but I've heard nothing about you."

"Did you move here with that asshole boyfriend of yours?"

"How do you know he wasn't my husband? Why are you assuming he was just a boyfriend?"

He smiled. "You weren't wearing a ring on the plane, and you're not wearing one now. The fact that you used past tense when you spoke about him leads me to believe that the two of you are no longer together."

"Mr. Young, would you care to explain to me how this has anything to do with this job interview?"

"Please, call me Simon. There's no need for formality here. And it doesn't have anything to do with the job interview. It's my curiosity that's getting the best of me."

Was he serious? "Fine. Then, let me put your curiosity to rest. He's not here with me. I left him and moved to Seattle. I'm staying with my best friend, Giana, for the time being."

"Smart girl," he said as he continued to look over my resume. "You graduated from Cornell with honors and in the top ten percent of your class. Very impressive. It looks like Holster Marketing's loss is my gain. I'm going to take a leap and call them fools for letting someone like you go."

"Thank you," I spoke as I looked down.

"You're not used to taking compliments, are you, Gabrielle?"

I couldn't believe the nerve of this man. Who the hell did he think he was? I looked at him and cocked my head.

"What makes you think that, Mr. Young?"

"Simon," he spoke as he leaned forward and put his hands on the desk. "You keep looking away from me. Do I make you uncomfortable?"

What I really wanted to tell him was, yes, extremely uncomfortable, but I couldn't risk not getting this job.

"No, not at all."

"Good. Because the last thing I'd want is for you to feel uncomfortable if you're going to work for me." He smiled.

"Really?" I asked as I looked at his left hand. He wasn't wearing a ring.

"Yes. I feel you're the perfect candidate for our marketing position. Can you start tomorrow?"

"Yes, and thank you, Mr.— Simon."

"That's better. If you'll excuse me, I'll bring Peter back in. I'm late for a meeting." He got up from his chair, and so did I. He walked over to me and extended his hand.

"Welcome to Young International, Gabrielle. It will be a great pleasure having you as an employee," he expressed with delight.

I had to know. I just had to. I blurted out as he opened the door, "You have a very beautiful wife."

He turned around and flashed his sexy smile at me. "She's not my wife. She's a friend, and yes, she is beautiful, but not as beautiful as you." He walked out the door and left me standing there speechless.

A few moments later, Peter walked in and shook my hand. "Congratulations, Gabrielle. Mr. Young seems to really like you," he said with concern.

"Thank you. He seems nice."

Peter laughed. "He's the boss, and what he says goes. I was going to hire you anyway. Go home and enjoy yourself today. I'll see you here in my office tomorrow morning at eight o'clock."

I nodded my head and walked out the door. As soon as I exited the building, I did a little dance on the sidewalk. I couldn't believe how fast I got a job, and to be working for Young International was huge. I pulled out my phone and dialed G.

"How did it go?" she answered.

"I got it! I got the job!" I squealed.

"Good job, Gabby. I knew you would."

"Thanks again for letting me use your car today. I guess I need to go look for one of my own."

"Don't worry about it yet. Donovan can drive me to the office for the rest of the week. Don't rush into buying anything today."

"Are you sure? Because I feel bad."

"Don't be silly. I love having Donovan pick me up."

"Okay. I'll see you later when you get home."

"Bye, Gabby."

I walked to the parking garage where G's car was parked, and as I pulled the handle to open the door, a black limousine pulled up, and the passenger window rolled down.

"Is that your car?" Simon asked as he studied the 2011 Subaru.

"No. It's my friend's car. She let me borrow it today for the interview."

"So you don't have one?"

"Not yet. I'm going to look for one this week." I smiled, even though I was irritated with his nosy questions.

"Give me your address." He grinned.

"Excuse me?"

"Give me your address, and I'll have my driver, Patrick, pick you up in the morning."

How many times did I have to ask myself if this guy was serious? "It's fine, Simon. She's letting me use her car until I get one."

"Gabrielle, there's one thing you will learn very quickly about me: I don't take no for an answer. I never have, and I never will," he spoke with seriousness.

I put my hands up. "Fine." I rattled off G's address, and with a smile, he thanked me and told me to have a nice day.

~

*A*fter shopping for new clothes, I stopped at the market and picked up some ingredients to make dinner tonight. It was the least I could do for G since she let me stay here and use her car. As I began to prepare the sauce for spaghetti, I heard the front door open, and it sounded like G was on the phone. She walked into the kitchen and held up a brown bag with a smile before setting it on the counter. I got the feeling she was talking to Donovan. Just thinking about him made me sick. When she hung up, she pulled out a bottle of wine from the brown bag.

"We are going to celebrate tonight with this beautiful bottle of wine." She smiled. "Congratulations on getting the job. I want to hear all about it."

"Then you better sit down," I said as I stirred the sauce. "Because you aren't going to believe what I'm about to tell you."

"Uh oh. This doesn't sound good." She bit down on her bottom lip and took her wine to the table.

"Oh, trust me. This is good. I interviewed today with the CEO of Young International."

"You mean Simon Young himself?" she asked.

"Yep. He's the one who hired me."

"That's odd. Usually, CEOs don't do that sort of thing."

"Exactly. But he walked in on Peter and me during our interview, kicked Peter out, and continued it himself."

"Fuck, Gabby. That man is hot. As in the sexy I-would-fuck-him-all-night-long-and-never-stop way."

I sighed. "He is sexy. Isn't he? But that's not the kicker. Are you ready?"

"Shit, Gabby. Spill it!"

"Simon Young was the man on the airplane when Brendon and I flew back from Vegas."

Her jaw dropped. "You mean the sexy guy that sat across the aisle from you and helped you with your bag? The same man you couldn't stop thinking about?"

"Yep. That's the one." I smiled.

"For the love of God, Gabby. Do you know who this man is?"

"No. I never even heard of him until today."

"Well, that's because you lived in a bubble with Dickwad in your own little world."

I shot her a look.

"He's thirty years old and is worth millions. His parents were killed in a train accident in London when he was just five years old, and he was sent to the States to live with his grandfather. Simon's father wanted nothing to do with the hotel industry or the company that his father had spent his entire life building from the ground up, so Simon's grandfather made it so Simon would be the one to take over when he died. He's not dead yet, but rumor has it he's on his way out, and when he does die, Simon will no longer be worth millions. He'll be worth billions. Billions, Gabby!"

"And?"

"What do you mean 'and'? It sounds to me like he's attracted to you."

"Don't be stupid, G. Someone like Simon Young would never be interested in me seriously. He's a playboy, I'm sure. All rich and powerful men are."

"Yeah. He is a playboy. According to reports, he has women worldwide and never wants to settle down."

"Good for him. I hope he enjoys all his women because the only thing I'm doing is working for his company. I'm earning a living and starting over. I'm done with rich guys. They're all alike. Give them money and power. They think they own the world and can treat people poorly."

"Maybe, but is it really fair to stereotype like that? I mean, just because you wasted six years of your life on Dickwad when I told you from day one that he was no good doesn't mean all rich men are like that."

I started to say something about Donovan but stopped myself. I would never listen to her when she talked about Brendon, and there was no way she'd listen to me, even though Donovan fit the rich man profile.

"Doesn't matter. I was fooled once, and I won't be fooled ever again. You know what Brendon did to me, G. You know how he stripped me of everything and anything good about me." Tears started to form in my eyes.

She got up from the table and wrapped her arms around me, giving me her best friend hug. "I'm sorry, Gabby. I'm so sorry about what he put you through, but him cheating on you and you finding him was the best thing that could've happened. Now we're together again, and you're going to be working for one of the largest and most prestigious companies in the whole world. Everything happens for a reason, babe." She winked.

Maybe she was right. Hell, if I knew. I was just going to take my life one day at a time, but this time, I was doing it the smart way.

"Oh, by the way, I don't need your car tomorrow. Simon is sending his driver to pick me up."

She nearly choked on the wine she was sipping. "What? He's picking you up?"

"Yep. He saw me get into your car, and he stopped and asked about it. I told him it was yours and that you were letting me borrow it. He insisted that his driver pick me up tomorrow."

"Oh, sweetie. You better hang on tight because your life is totally about to change."

"You're right. It is, and I'm the one making the changes. Good changes. Changes for me and me only. This is my life, G, and nobody will ever control me again."

Chapter Eight

My alarm went off before the sun came up, and I was already starting to feel extremely nervous. It was hard enough having to start a new job and meet new people, let alone having the CEO of the company send his driver to pick me up for work. After putting on my makeup and straightening my hair, I slipped into my black boot-cut dress pants and a black and white cami. I grabbed the matching black ruched-sleeve jacket from the closet and put it on. I heard a whistle from behind.

"Looking sexy in that outfit, G. Are you trying to look hot for Simon?" She smirked.

"No, and I'm not hot. So stop saying that."

"I don't care if you think you are or aren't. I say you are, so you are," she said as she sipped coffee from her mug.

I shoved my feet into a pair of black heels and took the coffee cup from G's hand.

"Hey."

"Sorry, I just need a few sips. I don't have time to make another cup."

As I entered the living room, there was a knock at the door. "Shit!" I exclaimed. "Why is he knocking on the door? I thought I'd meet him downstairs," I whispered.

"Relax," Giana said as she opened the door and invited Patrick in.

"Good morning, Miss McCarthy. Are you ready to go?"

I took in a long, deep breath before answering. "Yes. I'm ready."

He held the door open, and we took the elevator down to the first floor, where I could see the limo parked at the curb from the front doors of the building.

Patrick was about five foot ten with a medium build and appeared to be in his mid-fifties. His brown hair was kept neat and short on the sides, with a good amount of balding on top. His round face and his deep brown eyes gave him a cuteness factor. When we exited the building, Patrick opened the limousine door, and I inhaled sharply as I climbed in and saw Simon sitting there, smiling at me.

"Good morning, Gabrielle. You look very nice today."

I sat down and looked at him, cocking my head as my eyes took in his presence. His masculine, sexy presence already had produced the familiar ache between my legs, not to mention the light musk smell that was radiating off of him.

"Good morning. Do you always pick up your new employees at their homes?"

He chuckled. "No. Actually, this is a first for me."

I gave him a small smile and looked out the passenger window. If I thought my stomach was a nervous wreck earlier, it just became ten times worse.

"Have you eaten breakfast?" he asked.

"No. I'm not hungry."

"Do you eat at all, Gabrielle?"

I looked at him and frowned. "Of course, I eat. Why would you ask me that?"

"Then show me," he smirked. "Patrick, pull into the next Starbucks. Miss McCarthy would like a coffee and a pastry."

I sat there in disbelief that he would do that. I was having flashbacks of Brendon, and it was making me angry.

"Actually, Patrick. Do not pull into the next Starbucks. I want nothing, and I refuse to be late for my first day of work."

"You're with the boss. You can be as late as I want you to be."

"I thought Peter was my boss, and he's expecting me at precisely eight o'clock. I will be there, in his office, at eight o'clock."

His lip curled. "Forget Starbucks, Patrick. Fine. Then you can prove to me that you eat by having lunch with me."

"Okay. I'll have lunch with you."

"Excellent. I'll stop by your office and pick you up."

"I have an office?" I asked innocently.

"Of course, you have an office. Didn't Peter show you?"

"No, he didn't. I'm sure he'll show me when I get there."

I honestly thought I was going to be sitting behind a desk in a cubicle like I did at my other firm. The thought of having my own office excited me. Patrick pulled up to the curb, got out, and opened my door. As I stepped onto the sidewalk, Simon walked next to me and held the door open. The one thing I didn't notice when I was here yesterday was the gold lettering that spelled Young International on the brick of the building next to the door. We stepped inside the glass elevator, and Simon hit the buttons for the sixteenth and twentieth floors.

"Is that the floor your office is on?"

"You could say that." He grinned.

I didn't know quite what he meant, but I just went with it. As we stood in the elevator, he kept his hands in his pockets the whole time. He stood with confidence and authority. I saw the way people stared at him when we walked into the building. How the women admired him and secretly stole discreet glances while he was in their sight. I watched the men push back their shoulders and smile, almost as if they were going to salute him like he was some kind of soldier. The elevator stopped on the sixteenth floor. Before stepping out, I thanked Simon for the ride into the office.

"Thank you for picking me up and bringing me to work."

His lips formed a smile. "You're welcome. Trust me when I tell you it was my pleasure. Have a good morning, Gabrielle, and I'll see you at noon for lunch."

I stepped out of the elevator and walked down the hallway to Peter's office.

"You're right on time." He smiled.

"Of course. Good morning."

He showed me around the office and introduced me to the rest of the marketing team before taking me to my office.

"This is your office. I hope you'll find it cozy. It's one of the best ones on the floor. Feel free to put whatever you want in here, and right outside your door is Katie. She's your secretary/assistant. I don't know where she is at the moment, but as soon as she gets back, I'll introduce you to her." He stepped out into the hall.

I stood there and looked around my new office. The taupe-colored walls were complemented by two oversized cherry-stained bookcases that sat behind my matching cherry wood desk. Over to the left was a glass table with a cherry wood frame on which a printer sat to the left, and a vase of beautiful yellow roses sat in the center. I walked over to the flowers and removed the small white envelope with my name on it that was propped up against the vase. I removed the card from the envelope.

"Welcome to Young International. I hope your job turns out to be everything you hoped it would be. ~ Simon Young."

I didn't know what to think about any of this. This office, these flowers. This was not normal for a marketing associate.

"Gabrielle, can you step out here for a moment?" I heard Peter say.

"Katie, this is your new boss, Gabrielle. Gabrielle, this is your secretary, Katie."

I extended my hand to her, and she smiled as she lightly shook it.

"I love your outfit," she said as she looked me over.

"Thank you."

I asked Peter if he could come into my office.

"Is something wrong, Gabrielle?"

"Yes. I'm completely confused about all of this. Since when does a marketing associate have an office and a secretary?"

He chuckled. "You're not a marketing associate. You're the marketing manager of this division. Didn't Simon tell you?"

The Secret He Holds

"WHAT?!" I exclaimed.

"Oh boy. He said you were too qualified and well-educated to be an associate, so he gave you this position."

"Was this position even available?" I demanded to know.

"Not exactly. It used to be Jasmine's job, but she wasn't meeting the expectations of the company, so Simon demoted her."

"Great. So you're telling me that he demoted her to give me her position?"

"Yeah. Listen, Gabrielle."

"Call me Gabby."

"I like you already, and I can tell we're going to be good friends, so I'm just going to come out and say it. Be careful. I think Simon has more intentions with you other than work."

"I'm starting to think that too, and I'm not interested."

"Well, just to let you know, nobody tells him no."

"Then I guess I'll be his first." I smiled.

"I left those files on your desk to look over. I'm going to head to my office. Do you want to do lunch later?"

I sighed. "I'm going with Simon. He'll be here around noon."

Peter smiled. "Good luck. We can do it another time."

I sat down at my desk and asked Katie to come in. She was a cute girl, and she looked to be about the same age as I was. She stood about five feet five inches tall with a size zero body, long, curly blonde hair, and green eyes with a hint of gold.

"Is there something I can do for you?" she asked with a smile.

"How long have you worked here?"

"About six months."

"I may need you to show me the ropes, so to speak."

Her face lit up with a wide smile. "Of course I will. You seem really nice, and I think I'll like working for you. Jasmine sort of went out of her way to be mean."

"I'm sorry to hear that."

"How do you take your coffee?" she asked.

"Black. Why?"

"Because every morning, I'll have coffee waiting for you."

"That's really sweet of you, but totally not necessary."

"I want to. It's part of my job."

My eyes diverted to the doorway where Simon was leaning against the frame with his arm above his head. The ache between my legs was back.

"Are you ready for lunch?" He grinned.

"Yes. Thank you, Katie. I'll see you after lunch, and we can go over a few more things."

"Very well. Have a nice lunch, Miss McCarthy."

"Gabby. You can call me Gabby," I said to her.

Simon smiled as she walked towards the door and moved out of her way. I saw the way she looked at him, and I could tell she was smitten. I put my purse over my shoulder, and as I walked out of my office, Simon put his hand on the small of my back, sending goose bumps throughout my body.

Chapter Nine

Simon took me to a place called Mistral Kitchen, which wasn't too far from Young International. We were immediately taken to a quiet table for two in the corner as soon as we stepped inside. Simon pulled out my chair for me as the hostess handed me a menu. He took the seat across from me and told her to tell our waitress that we would like two glasses of white wine. I couldn't help but smile at him because he remembered my drink from the plane.

"White wine is fine, correct?" he asked.

"Yes." I nodded.

As I looked over the menu, I had to keep reminding myself that this was a business lunch. The waitress set our glasses of wine down and proceeded to take our order. I ordered first and couldn't help but stare at him as he looked over the menu. He was a man beyond any woman's wildest dreams in the looks department. After he placed his order, I decided to ask him about my position.

"Why didn't you tell me that you hired me as a

marketing manager? I was under the impression I was hired as an associate."

His lip curled as he began to speak. "You'll make a better manager. It's what I decided."

"I don't have any managerial skills, and what if it's not what I wanted?"

"What's not to want? Your salary is double. You'll get a monthly bonus and a company car. Not to mention the best healthcare benefits, including dental and vision. Plus, you have an office with a window."

"A company car?"

"Yes. A company car. One will be waiting for you when you get home." He grinned. "As for your managerial skills, you'll figure it out. I have faith in you. Plus, I talked to your ex-boss, Kendra. She raved about you."

I could feel the heat rise in my cheeks, so I looked down to avoid any embarrassment.

"Are there any other perks I should know about?"

He took a sip of his wine. "Only if you want there to be." He winked.

My stomach started twisting in a knot, and my palms began sweating. Why was he doing this to me? I needed to calm down and stay strong.

"Have you ever stayed at one of my hotels?" he asked.

"No. I'm sorry to say I haven't."

"Then maybe we'll have to take care of that. If you're going to work for me, then you should at least become familiar with the hotel. Perhaps the one where the gala was held. I'm sorry about that night. I was about to come over to you and tell you how beautiful you looked, but a business associate of mine needed me. So I'm going to tell you now. You looked incredibly beautiful that night. In fact, from what I can see, you're beautiful every day."

My heart was racing, and I didn't know what to say.

The Secret He Holds

My already heated cheeks were now on fire. I looked down first before picking up my glass and taking a sip of wine.

"Thank you."

"You're welcome."

The waitress came by and set our plates in front of us. I picked up a piece of my tomato, basil, and fresh mozzarella pizza and took a bite. "See? I eat." I smirked.

"I see that. Good to know."

It had been bothering me why he would even say something like that to me in the first place, so I asked him.

"Why do you think I don't eat?"

"Because your ex-boyfriend deterred you from eating a chocolate bar on the plane, and then he insulted you by comparing you to other women. Look at you. You're a what? A size four? Don't get me wrong, but from what I can tell, you have an amazing body. I just want to make sure you're not starving yourself."

I sat there speechless. It was highly inappropriate for him to be commenting on my body.

"You saw and heard that on the plane?" I asked.

"Of course I did. That asshole has a big mouth. I'm sure everyone on the plane heard."

"You're right. I am a size four because I eat healthy, and I work out."

"There's nothing wrong with indulging in sweets every now and again." He smiled as he took a bite of his food.

"And I find it highly inappropriate for you to be talking about my body. You're my boss, and I do believe that's a form of sexual harassment," I spewed.

"See it as you wish, Gabrielle. But I like looking at your body clothed, and I would like to see more of it unclothed." He winked.

Jesus, my panties were soaked. No one had ever talked to me like that before. I didn't know what to think. I was angry but turned on at the same time. *Strong. Stay strong*, I kept chanting in my head.

"I'm not sorry to say that my naked body is something you'll never see."

"We'll see about that." The corners of his mouth curved up into that sexy smile that I'd been seeing way too much for one day.

"Are we finished here? I need to get back to work."

The ride back to Young International was silent. Patrick smiled at me as he opened the door and helped me out. Simon walked a few feet behind me into the building, and I was very uncomfortable, for I knew he was checking out my ass. We stepped into the elevator, and I pushed the button to the sixteenth floor.

"By the way, I don't think I mentioned that I like what you did with your hair. It's very attractive on you," he spoke as he took a few strands in between his fingers.

I didn't say a word. I just shot him a look, and I stepped off as soon as the elevator doors opened. Before they had the chance to shut, I heard him yell, "You're welcome."

"Asshole," I mumbled under my breath.

～

Sitting down at my desk, I looked around my office. An office that needed a woman's touch.

"Katie, can you please come in here?" I yelled from my chair.

"You know there's an intercom button on the desk phone."

"Oh," I replied as I looked at the black multi-line phone sitting on the desk.

She laughed. "Did you need something?"

"Do you have a car?"

"Yes. Why?"

"Then come on. You're driving, and we're going shopping."

A big smile spread across her face. "Are you serious?"

"Yes. I need help sprucing up this office."

I grabbed my purse and walked down to Peter's office. "Hey. I'm going to take Katie, and we're going shopping for some things for my office. I'll be back in a bit."

"Uh. Okay. But you know we have catalogs for that stuff, and it'll be delivered," he replied.

"That's okay. I'd rather pick things out in person."

Katie and I climbed into her yellow VW Bug and drove to a store that was all about feng shui. I was reading up on it over the last couple of months. Thinking that maybe if I applied it to my home and love life, Brendon and I would be better together. Since I never got around to using it in New York, I figured, what better time to start. The fact that I was putting my past behind me and starting a new life made this the perfect time to put it into action. I spoke with the expert at the store and described my office. He made many wonderful suggestions about mirrors, artwork, and live plants. After spending a good hour with him, I made my purchases, and he would send it out for delivery tomorrow morning. Two of his people would come and set up my office in the energizing and productive feng shui way. I even picked up a couple of things for Katie's desk and area.

As we were driving back to the office, I decided to interrogate Katie about Simon.

"What are your thoughts on Mr. Young?" I casually asked.

"I have dirty thoughts. Very, very dirty thoughts about

what I'd like to do to that man in the bedroom," she spoke with seriousness.

"Okay. Tell me how you really feel." I laughed.

She sighed. "He's a womanizer. He has all the power and can have any woman he wants. All he has to do is snap his fingers, and women are at his beck and call. I've heard he has women around the world."

"Sounds like a total douchebag to me."

"I think he has a thing for you." Katie looked over at me. "I saw the way he looked at you today when he came to pick you up for lunch. He gave you that sexy glare of his. The glare that I would die to have on me."

"Down, girl!" I smiled.

"Want to know something else I heard about him?"

"What?"

"I heard that he's a freak in the bedroom. A good kind of freak. The kind of freak that makes your body feel good for weeks."

I put my hand up. "Okay. I've heard enough."

Katie laughed as we pulled into the parking garage. We took the elevator to the sixteenth floor, and I told Peter we were back. When I walked into my office, I looked around and couldn't wait until tomorrow morning for the feng shui people to come and redo my office.

Chapter Ten

*I*t was seven o'clock. G texted me and told me not to wait for her for dinner because she was working late. I rolled my eyes because her working late was code for "I'm with Donovan." I walked to the fridge and searched for something for dinner. It was pretty bare since neither of us had been grocery shopping. When I opened the freezer, I noticed there was a Lean Cuisine sitting there. I pulled it out, read the cooking directions, and popped it in the microwave. I picked up my phone from the counter when I heard the sound of a text message come through. It was from a number I didn't recognize.

"Are you decent? Can you come downstairs? I have something to show you."

It took me a minute to realize that it was Simon. Who the hell else would ask me if I was decent? I slipped on my Vans and took the elevator down to the lobby. As soon as the doors opened, Simon was standing in front of the elevator. He greeted me with that sexy smile.

"You didn't reply."

"I didn't think I had to. You told me to come down, so here I am."

"We'll discuss that later, but for now, I want to show you your company car."

He held the door open for me. Sitting at the curb was a white convertible Mercedes Benz.

"Simon. No way. No way. No way," I said as I shook my head.

"This is your company car. Do you like it?" he asked with a wide grin.

"Umm…who wouldn't like this?" I lightly ran my hand across the hood of the car.

"Get in the driver's seat and take it for a ride. But be careful because it's very powerful. When you ride on a powerful thing, you must use caution until you get the feel of it. Test it out. Go slow and then fast. Push it to the grind and take it all in. Enjoy the ride, and let it excite you."

I looked over at him as he sat in the passenger's seat. "You are talking about the car, right? Because I think you meant to say when you ride *in* a powerful thing, not on."

He snickered. "Of course."

I rolled my eyes, and I found my heaven the minute I sat down inside. The plethora of comfort was astounding as my body sank into the leather seat.

"Push this button right here."

I pushed in the button Simon pointed to and flinched as the seat took hold of my back, enveloping me in a deep massage.

"What the hell!" I looked at Simon.

"It's a hot stone massage. It's for when you've had a tough day, and your back is hurting. Just push that button and let the car work its magic. Unless you'd rather I give your back a massage. I guarantee that could be arranged."

I took in a deep breath—another pair of panties was on the verge of becoming soaked.

"No, thank you. I'd rather have the car do it."

"Then start her up and take it for a spin."

I looked over and motioned for him to get out with my hand.

"You don't want me to go with you?" he asked in confusion.

"No. I would like a little privacy, please."

"Suit yourself. Have fun." He climbed out and shut the door. "I'll be waiting right here."

Once again, I rolled my eyes and took off. I threw my head back and smiled as the cool breeze swept across my face. The speed and calm vibration of the car were amazing. I drove around the area a couple of times and then pulled into a parking space outside my building. Simon stood on the sidewalk with a smile on his face. He walked over and opened the door for me. I will admit one thing. He was a gentleman in that way.

"Do you love it?"

"I do." I smiled. "Thank you."

His eyes stared into mine for a brief moment. "You're welcome, Gabrielle. Do you mind if I come up and use your bathroom?"

"Is that your way of trying to get into my apartment?"

He chuckled. "No. I'm being serious. I really do have to go."

"Sure. Come on up. It's down the hall and to your left," I said as we entered the apartment. "Oh shit, my dinner." I walked over to the microwave and took out the cold Lean Cuisine.

Simon entered the kitchen and looked down at it. "That's what you were having for dinner?"

"It's all we have at the moment. I had just put in the microwave when I got your text message."

"I'm sorry that I distracted you from eating whatever that is. I'll make it up to you by buying you dinner now. We can either go out or order in." He smiled.

I was hungry. I hadn't eaten a thing since lunch, and anything sounded better than that Lean Cuisine. Being alone with him in my apartment was too risky. I didn't trust him not to try something.

"There's this diner right around the block that I've been wanting to try. G says they have the best tuna melts."

"G?" He cocked his head.

"Giana. My best friend. I call her G. I have ever since we first met."

"Cute. Let's go get a tuna melt," he said as he opened the door.

"Welcome to Sam's Diner. What can I get you?" the dark-haired waitress asked as she snapped her gum.

"I'll have the tuna melt and fries, please." I smiled as I closed the menu.

"And for you, hot stuff?"

It would only be a matter of seconds before I busted out into laughter.

"I'll have the same," Simon said as he handed her his menu.

The moment she walked away, the laughter that I tried so hard to hold back escaped. I put my hand over my mouth.

"I know you're laughing at her comment. She's a little rough around the edges. Wouldn't you say?"

"Do you normally eat at these kinds of places?" I asked.

"No."

"Brendon wouldn't either." I looked down as I took the straw wrapper between my fingers.

"Do you miss him?"

I hesitated for a moment and then looked out the window at the busy city. "No. We had a lot of problems."

"You mean *he* had a lot of problems. Because what I saw from him on the airplane was completely inexcusable."

"Can we please not talk about him?"

"Of course. I apologize."

The waitress set our plates down in front of us and shot Simon what I presumed was her sexy look. Laughter escaped me again.

"I'm sorry," I said as I took a bite of my sandwich.

He sighed. "No need to be. I'm used to it." He winked.

"I'm sure you are." I smiled as I popped a fry in my mouth.

"You have a beautiful smile, Gabrielle, and don't ever let anyone tell you differently."

I pursed my lips, and once again, I looked down. When he complimented me, it made me uncomfortable. It wasn't right. Hell, would it ever be right from anyone? Brendon made me so self-conscious that I couldn't even accept a compliment.

"You can call me Gabby." The words just flew out of my mouth.

He gave me a small smile. "If you don't mind, I like Gabrielle. It's sophisticated."

We finished our sandwiches and walked back to the apartment building. "How are you getting back to your house?" I asked.

"I'll call Patrick," he replied, pulling out his phone.

"Then I'll wait with you."

I don't know why I said I would. Simon Young had grabbed my attention from the moment I saw him on the plane, and even three months later, he still had it. But he wasn't the type of man I was looking for if I was even looking. He was just another rich man who wanted to hold all the power and control over everything in his life. He was the type of man who would use people to get what he wanted, and I had the feeling he wanted me. To him, it was harmless flirting, but to me, it was harmful, not only emotionally but physically as well. I had to make a promise to myself not to succumb to him, no matter how hard he tried. Because, damn, he was already trying. I would never trust another man again after what Brendon did to me. I could never believe that anyone would ever be capable of loving me. Love was a need that consumed me, and look where it got me the first time—six years of my adult life spent living in the shadows of someone who pretended to love me. Someone who got off on tearing me down and tearing me apart. I was too vulnerable and too weak, and the last thing I needed was to fall in the arms of someone who was more than capable of hurting me again.

Chapter Eleven

We took a seat on the wooden bench outside my apartment building while Simon waited for Patrick to pick him up.

"Tell me about Gabrielle McCarthy."

"There isn't enough time." I softly laughed.

"I have all the time in the world to listen to you," he softly spoke as he tilted his head and looked at me.

"Maybe another time." A small smile escaped my lips.

"Then tell me one random thing about you. Just one."

"I have a photographic memory."

"Really? That's pretty cool."

"How about you? Tell me something random about Simon Young that the world doesn't know." I smiled.

He sighed. "Let me think. The world knows just about everything. Ah, I know. Now, don't laugh."

"I would never."

"I secretly like tea."

"What?" I laughed.

"You promised you wouldn't laugh."

"I'm sorry, but why would you not admit that you like tea?"

"Because tea isn't a man's thing."

"Who says?"

"Men." He chuckled.

Just as I was about to say something, Patrick pulled up to the curb. Simon stood and took hold of my hand, helping me up from the bench, but he didn't let go.

"Remember, that stays between us."

The warmth that filled my body by the touch of his hand felt amazing, yet it scared me.

"Your love for tea will never escape these lips."

"And what beautiful lips they are. Good night, Gabrielle." He let go of my hand and climbed into the limo.

As soon as he shut the door and pulled away, I whispered, "Good night, Simon."

Before reaching the lobby of my apartment building, I heard G call my name.

"Was that a limo that just pulled away?" she asked.

"That was Simon Young."

"And what was he doing here?" She pushed the button to the elevator.

"He brought me my company car, and then we went around the corner to that diner."

"Oh! Did you get the tuna melt?"

"I did, and it was very good."

She hooked her arm around me as we stepped off the elevator. "I'm proud of you."

"Thanks." I smiled as I laid my head on her shoulder.

∼

The Secret He Holds

I arrived in the office at approximately seven fifty-five.

"Good morning, Katie." I smiled.

Despite not getting any sleep last night because of one Simon Young, I was in a great mood.

"Morning, Gabby. One coffee coming right up."

I smiled and walked into my office. The feng shui people were due to arrive around eight-fifteen. Katie walked in and set my coffee on the desk.

"Thank you. I needed this." I sighed.

"Anything wrong?"

"No. I just didn't get much sleep last night." I turned on my computer and moved the files over to the other side of the desk.

She sat down in the plush black chair across from my desk. "Why? Were you having dreams about Mr. Young? I know I did." She swooned.

"No dreams." I laughed. "Just a bit restless. So much has happened in such a short period of time. It's hard to really believe it and process it all."

"I get that."

There was a soft knock on the frame of the door, and when I looked up, I saw a man and a woman standing there.

"Can I help you?"

"Miss McCarthy, I'm Greta, and this is Marty. We have your delivery and are here to feng shui your office." She smiled.

"Ah. Come in."

Katie got up from the chair and went back to her desk. Greta and Marty stepped inside the office with their notepads and looked around.

"Hmm," Greta mumbled. "This is all wrong."

"All I feel is blockage," Marty spoke.

"We're going to need to move that desk and those bookcases. Can you call maintenance to come up, please?" Greta asked.

I walked over to Katie's desk and asked her to give maintenance a call.

"Tell them it's urgent, and they need to come up right away."

"I'm on it, boss." She grinned.

Before walking back into my office, two men walked in with the items I purchased yesterday, and maintenance followed behind. Before I knew it, bookcases were being moved, and so was my desk. As I stood in the doorway and watched, a familiar voice spoke behind me.

"What's going on here?" Simon asked.

I jumped because he scared the shit out of me. "You scared me. You just can't sneak up on people like that."

"I apologize, but I wasn't sneaking up. What would you like me to do? Yell your name from down the hall to alert you that I'm coming?"

"Yeah, maybe you should. Anyway, good morning."

"Good morning. Now, what is going on in there?"

"It's called feng shui."

"You hired people to feng shui your office?"

"Yes. It'll be good for me. The minute they walked in, they said they could feel nothing but blockage." I looked back at Simon. He rolled his eyes.

"You really believe in that stuff?"

"Did you just roll your eyes at me?" I asked.

"Yes. You roll your eyes at me all the time. ALL.THE.TIME.

I couldn't argue with him on that one because it was true.

"As soon as your office is done, I need to see you in my office."

"About?"

"You'll find out when you come up. Twentieth floor."

"Okay."

His hand discreetly touched the small of my back, and I held my breath. I could feel the softness of his fingers through the silk shirt I was wearing. An hour later, my office was finished.

"Can you feel the energy and positivity flowing through this room?" Marty asked.

"Sure," I said as I looked at Katie and saw her laughing.

I thanked them for coming and sat down at my newly positioned desk. The office looked bigger and way better, especially with the two large plants that sat in opposite corners. I picked up the phone and asked Katie to call Simon and have him come down to my office. I wanted him to see my new space.

"I thought I told you to come up to my office," he said with irritation when he arrived.

"I wanted you to see my new space. Can't you just feel the energy and positivity flowing through the room?" I smiled as I placed my hands on my desk. "Isn't it much better?"

"If you like it, then that's all that matters. I personally don't believe in that horseshit but to each his own."

"Why the attitude, Simon?"

"Gabrielle, I asked you to come to my office, and you didn't. Instead, you had your secretary call my secretary to have me come down here."

"And look, you're here."

Simon took in a sharp, irritated breath. "You have two

days to prepare for a marketing meeting in Vegas. The file is up in my office, and I'll have Katie bring it to you."

"Two days? Vegas?"

"Yes. We'll leave on Thursday night. The meeting is on Friday, and we'll be back in Seattle on Sunday. You need to learn the ropes." He walked out of my office without saying another word.

I sat there, confused. Was he really that pissed that I didn't go up to his office? Was he that much of a control freak? Shaking my head, I turned my chair around and looked out the window. What the fuck did I get myself into, and why was he making me go to Vegas so soon?

Katie set the file on my desk, and I asked her to shut the door on her way out. I didn't want to be disturbed since I only had two days to prepare for a meeting I knew nothing about. As I opened the file and studied it, it seemed that Young International was looking to renovate a lower-class hotel. But why? After a few hours, Katie walked into my office with a salad from the café down the street. After I finished eating, I walked down to Peter's office, only to discover he wasn't in today.

It was five o'clock, and Katie slowly opened the door and poked her head in.

"Gabby, I'm leaving for the night. I'll see you in the morning."

"Okay. Have a good night, and thanks for all your help today."

"No problem."

She left the door open, and I continued to look over the enormous file Simon had given me and put together a proposal. While I was engrossed in my work, I heard someone clear their throat. I looked up and saw Simon standing in the doorway.

"What are you still doing here? It's seven o'clock."

"Working," I said as I looked back down at the papers.

He walked in and took the seat across from my desk. "I didn't mean for you to overwork yourself."

"Why are you here, Simon?"

"Excuse me?"

"My office is horseshit, remember? You couldn't get out of here fast enough earlier."

"First of all, I didn't say your office was horseshit. I said that feng shui is horseshit, and you made me mad earlier."

I closed the file, hit the print button on my computer, and got up from my seat to collect the papers I had printed. I couldn't look at him because I was still pissed about earlier in the day, and I didn't like that he called feng shui horseshit. I took the papers from the printer and put them in a manila folder. I threw the folder down in front of him.

"My two days of preparation are done. Thanks to what you call horseshit." I grabbed my purse, and before I walked out the door, I turned and looked at Simon.

"Have a good night, Mr. Young."

Chapter Twelve

When I arrived home, I heard noises coming from the kitchen. I set down my purse, and when I walked in, I was privy to Donovan and G's make-out session on the kitchen counter.

"Really? You have a bedroom right down the hall."

"Hi, Gabby." Donovan smiled.

"You're just in time for dinner," G said as she hopped off the counter.

"I don't want to interrupt the two of you. I'll just take mine to the bedroom."

"Like hell, you will. You're going to sit down with us." She reached into the cabinet and took down an extra plate.

Donovan was kind enough to pour me a glass of wine.

"You look like you had a rough day," he spoke as he handed me the glass.

"To say the least. Oh, by the way, I have to go out of town on a business trip. I'm leaving Thursday and returning on Sunday."

G's eyes lit up like fireworks lit up the sky. "A business trip? Is Mr. Young going?"

"Yes. Unfortunately."

"Where are you going?" Donovan asked.

"Vegas."

"Well, at least you're going with a human being this time. Make sure to have plenty of sex while you're there," G said as a smile splayed across her face.

"It's for a business meeting, and there will be no sex. Knock it off with that. Plus, you couldn't pay me enough to have sex with Simon."

"Who said anything about Simon? Hook up with some random hot stranger. Someone you'll never see again. It's magical, I'm telling you." She winked.

Donovan glanced over at her and raised his eyebrow. "And you know this how, darling?"

"Because I've done it. What did you think? I was some goody-two-shoes virgin before I fucked you?"

I put my hands over my ears. "Stop."

The three of us sat down and ate dinner. I couldn't help thinking about Donovan's wife and what excuse he gave her for not being home. I decided to be bold and ask because Simon had already put me in a pissy mood.

"So, where's your wife tonight, Donovan?"

"Gabby!" G exclaimed.

"She's visiting her sister in Portland. She'll be back on Sunday."

I did have to give them some credit. At least they weren't fucking at his house in the bed that he and his wife shared—unlike some men I knew. I took my plate to the dishwasher and told Donovan and G good night.

"Donovan's spending the night. We'll try to keep it down."

"Okay," I replied with a fake smile.

After changing into my pajamas, I heard my phone

ding. I walked over to the nightstand, and when I picked it up, I was shocked to find a text message from Simon.

"Be in my office tomorrow morning at exactly eight o'clock."

I sighed as I replied.

"Okay."

"Okay? That's all you're going to say?"

I climbed under the covers and propped myself up against the headboard.

"Master?"

"Very funny, Gabrielle. Sleep tight, and I'll see you in the morning."

"Okay."

"?"

"Master?"

I couldn't help but smile. He didn't reply back, so I was sure I pissed him off. I set my phone down and drifted off to sleep until I was awoken by the grunts and moans of two people down the hall. I pulled the pillow over my head and tried to go back to sleep. Before I knew it, the alarm went off, and I could barely get out of bed.

~

*S*hit. *Shit. Shit.* I ran into the building and saw someone getting on the elevator. "Hold that door," I yelled.

I thanked the nice man and looked at the time on my phone. It was 8:01. *Shit.* I pushed the button to the twentieth floor. The elevator stopped on the tenth floor, and as soon as the man exited, I pushed the close button like a wild animal. Finally arriving on the twentieth floor, the doors opened, and I was immediately greeted by a beautiful redhead behind a large cherry wood desk.

"Is he in there?" I asked as I ran past her.

"Yes. Good luck," she said.

I stopped as I got to the door and took in a deep breath. As I turned the knob and lightly pushed it open, I saw Simon standing behind his desk, looking out the enormous window.

"You're late," he said without even turning around to see who it was.

"Sorry. I had a rough night."

"So having a rough night is an excuse to be late? And why was it so rough? What happened?"

"It's hard to get any sleep when your roommate and her married boy toy are fucking nonstop all night."

That caught his attention. He turned around and looked at me with a sly grin. "Did it make you horny?"

"Excuse me?" The nerve of this man and the things that flew out of his mouth.

He slowly slithered his way over to where I was standing, his hands in his pockets and a fire in his beautiful eyes. He looked way too damn sexy in his expensive black suit.

"Did you touch yourself?" He lightly placed his finger under my chin, and suddenly, I was frozen.

I gulped. "No."

"Why not? Didn't it excite you in the least to hear two people having sex so close to you?"

I gulped again. "Maybe."

"Then why didn't you touch yourself?"

I snapped out of my trance. This was none of his business, and he was making me uncomfortable. At least my mind was uncomfortable. I couldn't speak for other areas of my body.

"I'm not discussing this with you any further. Now, why did you summon me here?"

He flashed his sexy smile at me, turned around, and went back to his desk.

"Coffee?" he asked.

"Please," I replied as I sat down.

He called his secretary, Nell, and told her to bring in two coffees.

"Your proposal was brilliant."

"Really?" I asked with a hint of excitement.

"Yes. I wanted to thank you for getting it done so quickly."

Nell walked in and handed me my coffee. "Thank you." I smiled.

She nodded, and after setting Simon's on his desk, she walked out, shutting the door behind her.

"No tea today?" I smirked.

"Very funny, Gabrielle. You look incredible today. I hope you plan on bringing a bikini to Vegas for when we go swimming."

"We're going swimming?"

"Yes. Just the two of us on the rooftop of my hotel."

He spoke so seductively that I couldn't help but bite down on my bottom lip when he said that.

"I'll bring my bathing suit, but I don't wear bikinis."

"When you're with me, you'll wear a bikini. So, if you don't have one, you can either go out and buy one before we leave, or we'll pick one up for you in the hotel shop."

"I don't feel comfortable in a bikini." *Shit.* Why did I tell him that?

"I told you I wanted to see more of your body, and I expect you to grant me that wish."

What? Who the hell says that? Damn it. As uncomfortable as he made me feel, I was utterly turned on. A heat wave crashed throughout my body, and I needed to cool off.

"We'll talk about that another time. I really need to go," I said as I got up from my seat.

"I'll be in meetings all day and out of the building. Patrick will pick you up tomorrow morning at eight-thirty."

"Wait a second. You said we weren't leaving until Thursday night."

"I changed my mind. I thought we could take the day and do things. We can do whatever you want to."

"The last time I was in Vegas, it totally sucked," I said. "And, honestly, I'm not looking forward to returning there."

"You're not with him anymore. This time, it'll be different. I promise."

I walked out of his office in a sweat. What was he doing to me? I couldn't let this continue. It's not right, and it's not fair. Fuck you, Simon Young.

When G heard the door open, she came bouncing through the living room carrying a square white box with a pink ribbon tied around it.

"This was delivered for you today." She smiled as she handed it to me. "Hurry, open it. I've been dying to see what's inside."

"Who's it from?"

"I don't know. Maybe there's a card inside," she said as she bounced up and down, clapping her hands together.

I removed the pink ribbon and carefully took the top off the box. I found a black and white bikini while unwrapping the pink tissue paper. I picked up the black bottoms with the white strings tied in a small bow on the sides and swallowed hard. G picked up the black top with matching white strings and a cute white bow in the center. There wasn't much to it.

"Oh my God, Gabby. Who sent you this? It's so fucking sexy." She smiled as she held the bikini top up to her.

Lying in the bottom of the box was a small white envelope. I picked it up and pulled out the card inside.

"I think you would look amazing in this. See you tomorrow. ~ Simon"

I shook my head as G ripped the card from my hand. She read it and then looked at me with an expression of shock.

"What the hell is going on between the two of you?"

"Nothing. Nothing is going on. He comes on to me like it's no big deal. He says things he shouldn't, making me uncomfortable ninety percent of the time I'm around him."

"And the extra ten percent?" she asked.

"Drop it, G."

She set the bikini top down and took my hand. "Listen, Gabby. I know you're not used to real men, and they can be scary, but Simon is real. Just go with the flow. Shit. I know you're freaked out because you're not used to someone wanting you like that. If you must, put a wall of defense around you and have fun. Tuck your emotions away in a neat little pile in the corner of your mind, and just let go! Use him. Fuck him with no strings attached. No emotions and no attachment. Just two people having great sex for fun. It's easy. I used to do it all the time before Donovan. Just don't feel. You already know what a playboy Simon Young is. Do you think he's going to get all emotional? No, he's not. Be like him, Gabby."

Oh my God, my head was spinning from her spiel. Just to shut her up, I agreed.

"Good girl. I'm so happy for you."

"I'm leaving tomorrow morning."

"I thought you weren't leaving until tomorrow night."

"He changed his mind."

"You'll have a great time, sweetie. Don't let what Brendon did to you affect the rest of your life. This is your time to go out and live. You're single. You're beautiful, and you're desired. Play it up and take it for all it's worth." She kissed me on the forehead. "I have to go. I'm meeting Donovan for dinner. I'll see you in the morning before you leave."

I gave her a small smile. "Have fun."

Chapter Thirteen

I took one last glance at my suitcase before I zipped it up. Looking at myself in the mirror, I ran my fingers through my hair and took in a deep breath. Was I ready for this trip with Simon Young? No. I wasn't. Why me? Why was he so interested in someone like me? I had nothing to offer him.

I had decided to Google him last night before I went to bed, and the hundreds of pictures that came up with him and all the different women sickened me. The women he was with were glamorous. They displayed confidence and empowerment as they dangled on his arm. What did he want with me? I was nothing like them. Do I go against everything I ever believed about love and use him for my own pleasure? I'd watched plenty of porn and read plenty of sex articles. But still, I was inexperienced. Did love even exist anymore?

"Are you okay?" G asked as she stood in the doorway of my bedroom.

I snapped out of my thoughts and turned around. "Yeah. I'm great," I said with a fake smile.

I grabbed my suitcase and headed to the door. She followed behind and hugged me.

"Good luck. I wish I could tell you to behave yourself, but I can't. I want you to be a naughty girl on this trip. Remember: one-night stand, even if it is with a man named Simon Young. Unleash your sexual goddess on some poor soul." She laughed.

"Thanks. I'll let you know how it goes."

There was a light knock on the door, and when I opened it, Patrick was smiling.

"Good morning, Gabrielle. Are you ready?"

"As ready as I'll ever be." I sighed as he grabbed my suitcase and walked out the door.

"Remember, Gabby. ROAR!" G yelled down the hall.

When I reached the limousine, Patrick opened the door, and I slid inside. Simon was on the phone, and he looked at me and smiled. After hanging up, he brushed a strand of hair from my face.

"Good morning. Did you pack the bikini I sent you?"

"Good morning, Simon. Yes, I did."

"Good. Now that I know that, my morning is complete."

"What time does our flight leave?"

"Whenever we get there." He grinned.

"I'm confused. What do you mean?"

"We're taking my private jet. Why are you confused?"

"I didn't know that you had a private jet. Why were you flying commercially to New York if you have a plane?"

"My pilot became ill and couldn't fly. So I caught the next flight out. It was one of the best flights of my life."

"If I had my own private luxury jet and then had to fly commercial, I wouldn't consider it one of my best flights," I said.

"Well, it was the first time I saw you. So I consider it

the best flight of my life." He smiled as he lightly touched my chin.

I turned away so he wouldn't see me blush. My heart picked up a rapid pace, and my palms were sweating again. His phone rang, and I glanced over at him when he answered it. It was the first time that I'd seen him dressed in something other than a suit. How he wore light beige khaki pants, a white Ralph Lauren polo, and dark brown Martin loafers made him look incredibly and equally sexy. The empty ache between my legs was now a constant feeling whenever I was near him. He conducted business on the phone the entire way to the airport. When we arrived, Simon ended his phone call and climbed out of the limo. As I slid out of my seat, he held out his hand.

"Let me help you."

Those words. The first words he had ever spoken to me. The words that had been etched in my mind since they escaped his lips.

"Thank you." I gave him a small smile.

"I have a feeling you'll be thanking me a lot on this trip." He winked.

I took a sharp breath because he never let go of my hand until we stepped on the plane. I had never been in a private jet before and was enthralled by the soft grey interior. The finest leather seats, dark wooden tables, and two long, curved couches on each side of the plane were incredible.

"Do you like it?"

"It's beautiful. Sure beats a commercial plane." I smiled.

He chuckled. "If you need to use the bathroom, it's towards the back and to the left, next to the bedroom."

"You have a bedroom?"

"Of course. I'd be happy to show you it if you'd like."

The Secret He Holds

My stomach started to flutter. I didn't want to see it because I had a feeling that if I walked in there, I wouldn't be walking out any time soon.

"No. That's okay. Maybe another time," I shyly spoke as I took a seat on the leather couch.

"There will definitely be another time, Gabrielle."

A flight attendant by the name of Lucy walked up to where Simon and I were sitting.

"Good morning, Mr. Young. Mimosas?" she asked with a flirty smile.

"Good morning, Lucy. This is Miss McCarthy, and yes, mimosas are fine."

She nodded her head and smiled at me. I couldn't help but notice how pretty she was. After delivering our drinks, Simon placed a breakfast order for both of us. I wasn't sure if I could eat because I was nervous about this trip. Simon leaned back on the couch and crossed his legs as he looked at me.

"I want to know more about you, Gabrielle."

"Why?" I blurted out without actually meaning to.

He raised his left eyebrow. "Because we're friends, and I like to know everything about the company I keep. Where did you grow up? What about your family?"

I looked down as I moved the silver heart ring I wore up and down my finger. I didn't want to tell him anything, especially how I grew up. If I did, that meant I was opening myself up, something I didn't want to do.

"I don't like to talk about my childhood. I'm sorry."

He placed his finger under my chin and gently lifted it so I was staring at him. "You can trust me."

I involuntarily laughed. "Trust? I trusted someone once, and he let me down. So I'm just going to say that trust is no longer in my vocabulary."

His eyes darkened. "Again, you can trust me. We're

going to be on this plane for two and a half hours. Now, you can either tell me about yourself or entertain me in other ways."

Swallowing hard, I took a sip of my mimosa, and against my better judgment, I began to speak of my childhood.

"My only family is Giana, and I grew up in Trenton, New Jersey. I never knew my mother and father. Apparently, I was abandoned at the hospital. My birth mother checked herself out and was never to be seen again. The nurse who was taking care of me in the hospital took me home with her and raised me for the first two years until she became sick and couldn't take care of me anymore. I was flipped from foster home to foster home due to cracks in the system until I was finally placed in the home where Giana lived."

A soft look swept across his face as he placed his hand on top of mine. Chills shot throughout my body as his thumb softly stroked my flesh.

"Darcy and Curt Dolby. Two names I'll never forget. Drugs, gambling, prostitution, and gang relations were part of their life at night. By day, they presented themselves as the perfect couple who took in lost and unwanted children. They only cared about the money the state paid them for keeping us. When I moved in, there was Giana and a boy named Louis. Unfortunately, Louis got caught up in a gang and shot and killed a convenience store owner. He was put in juvenile detention until he was eighteen. After a string of robberies and a couple of rape charges, he was sent to prison, where he still resides. I had only known him for a couple of weeks. Once he was gone, it was only Giana and me. We bonded instantly and have been like sisters ever since."

"What happened to her family?"

"She never knew her dad and her mom was murdered. The state couldn't find any record of any other family, so she ended up with the Dolby's. We protected each other and practically raised ourselves."

Lucy set our breakfast trays down in front of us, and I asked her for some tea. Simon looked at me and smiled.

"I'll have some too, Lucy. So they made a living off drugs and prostitution?" he asked as he spread some jelly on his toast.

I nodded. "A shed in the back of the house had a mattress on the ground. That's where it all happened, every night."

"Did either one of them ever hurt you?" he asked with a darkness in his eyes.

"No. Aside from their way of living, they weren't mean people. At least not to us. They made sure we had clothes on our backs and a roof over our heads. I was the one who learned to cook, and I usually cooked dinner for all of us, including all their friends who popped in and out all the time."

"Do you keep in touch with them?"

"Nah. When I was sixteen, I was emancipated, and that really pissed them off. G had just left for college, and I didn't want to be alone in that house. She helped me with the process. Ever since her mom was murdered, she always wanted to get into law."

"How on earth did you live on your own at sixteen?"

"I stayed with G and a guy friend of hers in an apartment off her college campus. I got a part-time job at a bookstore and graduated with honors right before I turned eighteen. Went off to Cornell in the fall and met Brendon," I said as I looked down.

"And now you're here working for Young International,

and you're with me. Things are looking up for you, Gabrielle." A smile splayed across his face.

"Yeah, I guess they are." I wasn't quite sure what he meant by 'here with him,' and I wasn't sure I wanted to know.

Just as I was going to ask him to tell me about his life, Lucy walked over to alert us that we were getting ready to land. I took in a sharp breath. Let the games begin.

Chapter Fourteen

As soon as we exited the plane, we climbed into a black limousine that drove us to Simon's hotel. The minute we pulled up to the curb, three men ran over, opened the doors for us, and took our luggage from the trunk.

"Good day, Mr. Young. Welcome back."

"Thank you. This is Miss McCarthy."

"Nice to meet you, ma'am."

God, I hated when people called me "ma'am." I gave a small smile, said hello, and then Simon inserted a key where the elevator took us to the top floor: the thirtieth floor. When the doors opened, I was in awe of the elegance that stood before me. It was the presidential suite, which was the entire floor.

"Wow, Simon. This is gorgeous."

"I bet you've never seen anything like it. Have you?"

"No. I haven't." I walked over to the window and gasped at the view of the city.

Suddenly, I felt two hands grab my hips from behind and his hot breath trailing along my neck. I stiffened.

"Relax, Gabrielle. I just want to be close to you. You're so beautiful," he whispered as his soft lips touched my skin." A moan escaped his throat as his grip tightened. "You're so fucking beautiful."

I was so turned on, and all I kept hearing was G's voice in my head, telling me to play the game. No attachment. Just sex. No emotion. Just sex.

"Simon," I whispered.

"Yes." His tongue slid along my neck and to the tip of my earlobe.

"We need to talk."

Kisses came to a halt. "Talk? About what?"

I loosened myself from his grip and began to walk across the room. "Stuff. Things. I don't know. There are things you don't know. Things I'm not comfortable talking about with someone like you."

"What's that supposed to mean?" He walked over to where I was standing and lightly ran the back of his hand across my cheek. "You can tell me anything."

My heart was pounding, and my body felt like it was engulfed in flames. I took his hand from my face. My intention was to let it go and walk away, but I couldn't. I liked the way his skin felt on mine.

"I'm not experienced."

"Gabrielle, are you talking about sex?"

I nodded my head.

"What did he do to you?"

"Nothing. Sex was awful. For six years, we did it the same way. Always him on top and with the lights off." I spoke nervously.

"Did he pleasure you?"

"I can't talk about this with you," I pleaded.

Simon sighed and wrapped his strong arms around me, pulling me into a tight and warm embrace.

"You have nothing to worry about with me. I'm going to ask you one question, and I want an honest answer," he said as he broke our embrace. "Look at me, Gabrielle."

I couldn't. I was too embarrassed and scared about what he was going to ask me.

"I'll ask you one last time to look at me." He lifted my chin. "Have you ever had an orgasm?"

Shit. Oh my God, how could he ask me that? All I could do was lie and nod my head. The truth was that I was pretty sure I had never had one. Brendon had nothing to offer, and he didn't care whether I did or not.

"I think you're lying," he said as his hands traveled up my floral mini skirt and his grip on my bare ass tightened. "You're wearing a thong. I need to see if your ass is as perfect as I think it is."

He turned me around and lifted up my skirt. The nervousness that consumed my body intensified, as did the ache between my legs. He took in a sharp breath as he got down on his knees, and his tongue glided along my skin. His hands firmly kneaded each cheek as he took my flesh lightly between his teeth.

"Fuck. It's even more perfect than I had imagined," he moaned.

Simon stood up and placed his hands on each side of my face, smashing his mouth against mine. Our first kiss. A kiss that was feral, not soft and tender. His strong tongue forced my lips to part so it could enter my mouth and meet mine. He bent down and picked me up, carrying me to the bedroom. He softly laid me down and turned me on my side as he faced me.

"I'm going to make you come," he whispered as his hand slid up my thigh and to the edge of my panties. "I hope you brought plenty of extra panties."

His finger pushed the cotton to the side as he felt the wetness that had escaped my body.

"Fuck. You're so wet and beautiful. Were you ever this wet with him?" he whispered softly as his tongue slid across my lips.

"No." I inhaled sharply as his finger dipped into me.

"Good." He smiled.

I was completely lost. His fingers played around inside me as he placed his thumb on my clit, stroking it softly, causing me to swell even more. The vibrations happening inside me were nothing I'd ever felt before. I moaned with pleasure as he moved his fingers in and out. My hands instinctively reached for his erection through the fabric of his pants. He was rock solid, and I wanted nothing more than to touch it, feel it, and take his entire length in my hand.

He reached his other hand over and removed mine from him. "This is all about you, baby. Not me. You will give me the greatest pleasure of all in due time. But right now, this time is for you."

I thrust my hips forward as his thumb pressed deeper onto my clit. The sweet sounds of pleasurable moans escaped my lips as my body was building for release.

"You're about to come, Gabrielle. Look at me. Stare into my eyes as you release yourself all over my fingers. I want to see you come. I want to hear you come. I want you to say my name as you give me what I want."

"What do you want?" I asked with bated breath.

"I want you to come so I can taste you." His voice was soft but commanding as his fingers played with me.

The ache that I'd felt between my legs every time I was near him was finally getting fulfilled. I was at my peak as I yelled his name, and my body shook with intense pleasure as I released myself, giving him what he craved.

"That's my girl." He pulled his fingers out and went down on me, first lifting up my skirt and ripping off my panties. His tongue slid up and down my clit and around my wet folds, causing me to squirm at the lingering pulsating sensations. "You taste so good. So perfect, Gabrielle."

When he finished, he brought his lips to mine and commanded that I lick them.

"Taste what I taste. Taste the pleasure I gave you."

I did as he asked, and after a moment of feral kissing, he got up from the bed and smiled. "Go clean yourself up, and we'll go get some lunch."

I lay there, exposed, as my skirt was still pushed all the way up to my stomach, and my soaked panties were lying next to me. I was unable to move from what he had just done to me. He walked out of the room and into the other bathroom across the suite. I got up from the bed, cleaned myself up. As I walked over to the closed door to the bathroom, I could hear the muted sounds of his moans. He was masturbating. But why? Why didn't he let me take care of him? A thousand reasons were going through my mind. Maybe he felt I wouldn't be able to pleasure him. Maybe it made him think twice when I told him how inexperienced I was. I didn't know, but I was upset—just another blow to my self-esteem. I bent down on the floor and unzipped my suitcase that was still sitting in the middle of the room. I heard the bathroom door open as I took out another skirt, a tank top, and a pair of panties.

"What are you doing?" Simon asked as he walked over to me.

After closing my suitcase, I stood up and turned to face him. "I'm changing clothes."

He smiled as he wrapped his arms around me and

pulled me into him, holding my head firmly against his chest and softly stroking my hair.

"How do you feel?"

"Fine," I replied.

He pulled back, cocked his head, and raised his eyebrow. "Fine? That's all? Just fine? I just gave you, I would assume, the best orgasm of your life, and all you can say is 'fine'?" he said with irritation.

"I heard you jacking off in the bathroom. Why didn't you let me take care of you? Do you know how that made me feel?" I asked as I turned away.

He lightly took hold of my arm and turned me around. "I told you that today was about you, not me. What part of that don't you understand? And why would that bother you?"

"Because it made me feel like you thought I couldn't get you off. You have no idea what Brendon has done to me, how he stripped me bare of any self-confidence because of the things he said to me. Making me feel like a worthless piece of shit every time we made love, which wasn't very often, by the way." Tears began to fill my eyes.

"Are you kidding? I get off just by looking at you. You don't even have to touch me, Gabrielle," he said in a controlled tone as he placed his hands on my hips. "Listen to me. You are to never give that fucking asshole another thought. Whatever he said to you is not true. Trust me, you will be getting me off soon enough. You will never have to fear anyone putting you down again. You're an amazing woman with an incredible ass and beautiful pussy, and later, I will explore more of your body. I already have the images in my head of how perfect and perky your tits are, and I'm looking forward to watching you strip out of your clothes in front of me for the first time."

God, he was exciting me again. I gave him a small

smile as he leaned over and kissed my lips. "So I'll ask you again. How do you feel?"

"Wonderful. Exhilarated. I feel like I'm on top of the world." I smiled.

He chuckled. "If you feel like that from my hand, imagine how you're going to feel when my cock goes inside you." He winked. I gasped. He smiled. "Now go change your clothes, and let's get out of here. I'll bring the suitcases to the bedroom."

Chapter Fifteen

We ate lunch at his hotel restaurant, which was located on the rooftop. It was a beautiful sight, overlooking the city. It was breathtaking, just like the rest of the hotel was. I was reveling in glorious pleasure from earlier, and I couldn't stop thinking about the things Simon had said to me. After we placed our order, I looked at Simon as he took a drink of his bourbon.

"How did you come to acquire all this?"

He set his glass down and smiled. "I normally don't talk about my personal life with anyone."

"Okay, then don't."

"Well, since you really want to know, maybe I'll tell you a little bit."

"It's up to you."

He leaned back in his chair and studied me, trying to figure out what I was doing. To be honest, I wasn't doing anything. The less I knew about him, the better off I'd be.

"Just answer me one question because I'm curious to know. "Why haven't you married? I mean, look at you. You're drop-dead gorgeous. You can have any woman in the world. You've been with countless women, you're incredibly rich, and yet you've never married."

He picked up his glass and finished off his bourbon, never taking his eyes off of me.

"George Clooney is fifty-three and just married. Why did he wait so long?" he replied.

"George Clooney was married before."

"No, he wasn't," Simon insisted.

"Yes, he was. He married his first wife when he was twenty-eight years old. It didn't last long; only about four years."

"Are you a Clooney addict or something? Do you have some secret obsession with him that I should know about?"

"He's hot, but no. Giana was obsessed with him. She knows every little detail about him."

"Ah, I see. Well, if he was only married for four years, then he waited another twenty-one years to marry his second wife."

"That doesn't answer my question." I sighed.

"You want me to be completely honest with you?"

"Yes, I do."

"I don't have time for things like that. My main focus is my company, and it's going to be even more my focus when my grandfather passes away. I've seen too many successful men lose because they tried to juggle a career and family. The wife ends up nagging him to death because he's never home while he's working late hours to keep the company successful. Meanwhile, the kids get out of control, the wife gets mad and is always yelling, and ultimately, he stays out later than he should, making excuses as to why he's not going home. A home he can't stand going to anymore."

The waitress set down another glass of wine in front of me, and I quickly took a sip.

"So he ends up fucking his secretary. The wife finds out. Divorces his sorry cheating ass and takes him for half of what he's worth, if not all," I spewed.

"Exactly! I couldn't have said it better myself."

"And you've seen this?" I asked.

"Of course I have. You need to remember who I am. I know and deal with successful corporate men around the world, and it's the same story. So there's your answer."

I held up my glass. "Cheers." I smiled.

"Does that upset you?"

"No. Why would it upset me? I was just curious. If you choose to spend the rest of your life going from woman to woman, that's your decision."

"I'm not sure I like the way you just said that." He arched his eyebrow at me. "You're making me out to be a man-whore. You can't have your cake and eat it too. There's no perfect balance between a healthy relationship and a career. The career always comes first."

"Sorry. I didn't mean to offend you."

There was the answer I was desperately seeking, straight from the horse's mouth. He didn't want to be tied down.

"So, then, it's just about sex?" I asked, not knowing if I wanted to know the answer.

"Men and women have needs. Why complicate things with the rules of a relationship? It should be about two people having fun without the strings attached."

Visions of G were running through my head. "I once wouldn't have believed that. But since Brendon, I couldn't agree more." I smiled.

"I'm glad to know we're on the same page." He held up his glass to mine. "Cheers."

"Cheers." Our glasses clanked together, symbolizing our agreement that we were only using each other for sex and nothing else. But the real question was: was I capable of playing along?

~

As soon as we got back to the room, Simon took a phone call.

"I have to meet a colleague of mine for drinks down at the bar. Will you be okay here by yourself?"

Seriously? He was just going to leave me sitting in the room? Typical fucking rich man.

"I'll be fine. I'm used to being by myself."

"Gabrielle," he said, putting his arms around my waist. With his lips dangerously close to mine, he whispered, "I won't be long, and then we'll have the whole night together. And I promise it will be well worth it."

"Okay, but I'm not staying in this room. I'm going down to the casino."

"To play some slots?" he asked.

"Sure." I smiled.

"Do you need some money?"

"I have my own money, Mr. Young." I tenderly kissed his lips and then walked away.

"I'm not sure you should be going down there alone."

"You don't think your own hotel is safe?" I asked.

"It's the people, Gabrielle, not the hotel."

"Don't you have security walking around?"

"Of course."

"Then why are you worried? I'll be fine. I can take care of myself. I've done so for the past twenty-four years."

"Don't leave this hotel. Do you understand me?" His tone was authoritative.

"Yes, master." I winked as I walked out the door.

I took the elevator down to the casino and headed to

the blackjack table first. I sat down at the only seat available. A seven-seat table where I was the only woman sitting.

"What's the minimum bet?" I asked the sexy dealer.

"Twenty-five dollars."

"Of course it is." I grinned.

It figured that Simon would have a high minimum in his hotel.

I took three hundred from my purse and set it on the table. Pushing it towards the dealer, I asked for three hundred in chips. He set them down in front of me, and the game began. I lost the first few hands and was down about two hundred dollars.

"Well, I guess this is all I have left," I said as I put my last hundred down.

The sexy dealer smiled at me as he distributed the cards, and I won. Doubling the bet, I won again. The third time was the charm as I got up from the table and walked away with a wad of cash. Time to move. Couldn't stay at a table for too long. I headed to the poker table. Two hours had passed, and Simon was still MIA. Flashbacks of times like these started flipping through my head when I was in Vegas with Brendon.

Just like blackjack, I lost the first few hands of poker. Steadily increasing my bets, I began to win—time to go back to the blackjack table. Pulling out only a hundred bucks, I took a seat and bought some chips. As I placed my bet, I felt two hands lightly grip my shoulders and a voice whispering in my ear.

"I thought you were playing slots."

"But this is much more fun." I smiled as I won.

"Are you ready to go back to the room?" he asked.

"No. I'm not done here. Why don't you have a seat and play," I said as I patted the chair next to me.

The Secret He Holds

"Fine." He sat down and pulled out a wad of cash.

Simon lost every hand he bet on. I won and won big. My bets increased with each win, and my time was up. I collected my chips and got up from my seat.

"I'm ready now." I smiled over at Simon.

He got up and placed his hand on the small of my back as he walked with me over to the cashier.

"That's an awful lot of money you won."

"It wasn't all from blackjack. I hit the poker table too." I grinned.

After cashing in my chips and walking away with five thousand dollars, he lightly took hold of my elbow and whispered in my ear, "I think you just ripped off my casino with that photographic memory of yours."

"How do you think I paid for part of my tuition at Cornell?"

"Unbelievable, Gabrielle. Just fucking unbelievable."

Chapter Sixteen

When we returned to the room, I took off my shoes and sat on the plush couch, checking my phone for any messages. I was surprised that G hadn't messaged me.

"Wine?" Simon asked.

"Yes, please."

"Tell me where you learned to play cards like that."

"I taught myself. Curt and Darcy would have poker games at the house at least three nights a week. I would sit and study them as they played. I started playing when I was sixteen with a bunch of college kids when I lived with G. There were secret poker games going on in the basements of the frat houses. Some were small, and some were big. When I attended Cornell, the pots and stakes were even higher because that was where all the rich kids went."

"You never got caught when you won so much?" he asked.

"I didn't win every time. If I did, that would make me look suspicious. That's why I would win big one time and make it look like a fluke and other times; I'd lose on purpose. I never stayed at the same place long enough to get caught. That's why I don't stay at the tables that long. I lose first, win, and move on to another table, then I stop completely. I can't have the casino catching on to me."

He looked at me with a small smile. "I'm honestly at a loss for words right now."

I looked down at my hands. "It's my little secret. The only other person who knows is G. I never told Brendon."

"Well, I'm honored that you told me." He leaned over and brushed his lips against mine. Our tongues met and danced as our lips moved in sync. He broke our kiss and placed one hand on my cheek. "You drive me crazy, Gabrielle." He took my hand, and we stood up. "It's time for me to see your entire body."

I became nervous but turned on at the same time.

"I bought you something, and I want you to put it on." He handed me a pink square box with a silver bow. "Go change in the bathroom, and I'll be waiting in the bedroom." His finger lightly traced my jawline and then the outline of my lips. He smiled and walked to the bedroom.

I took the box into the bathroom and lifted the lid. I removed the garment from the box, and my heart started to race. It was a sheer black baby doll nighty with a front hook, eye closure, and ribbon. Inside the box sat a matching V-string panty. I stared at myself in the mirror as I stripped out of my clothes and into the baby doll nighty and panties. The front of the outfit was open down the middle, showing my bare skin. I tied the little bow and took in a deep breath. This was it. I tried to play it off in my mind as no big deal. Simon Young turned me on countless times and left me with nothing but fantasies. My fantasy would come true, and I needed to prepare myself for the consequences.

Walking to the bedroom, I noticed the door was slightly closed. I lightly knocked, and Simon told me to come in. When I stepped in, I struggled for breath when I saw him sitting in his khakis in the oversized leather chair in the corner of the room. Shirtless and barefoot, he overwhelmed me. His broad shoulders sat back against the chair as his chiseled six-pack stared straight at me.

"Stop right there," he commanded as he held a glass of bourbon in his hand. His gaze was pure and steady. "Turn around for me."

I turned around and heard the sharp intake of his breath. "Now turn back around." His eyes were full of delight as his lips slowly parted. "Come here. I want to feel your body in that before you take it off."

I slowly walked over to the chair. He sat straight up and placed his hands on my hips. His tongue slid across my stomach in long, smooth strokes as he moved his hands up and down my sides, taking in the sheer feel of the fabric. He gently turned me around and cupped my ass in his strong hands. He placed his mouth on my bare flesh, where he nipped and then licked the spot to soothe the sting. I felt his hand cup my pussy as soft moans rumbled from his chest.

"It's time for me to see those perfect tits of yours. Go back over there and slowly strip out of that nighty."

He had me so turned on and wanting him that I could barely control myself. I felt like he was torturing me for his own pleasure. I walked across the room and faced him. After slowly untying the bow, I let down one strap of the nighty. After unhooking the eye, I deftly let go of one cup and let it fall, exposing my bare breast. I watched him gulp. I could see his erection through his pants from across the room. I released my other breast from the nighty, which was barely hanging on, and let it fall to the ground. My heart was pounding to escape my chest, and my body was overheating. I'd never done this before, and my knees were steadily shaking. Simon got up from the chair with a gaze that was fixated on my breasts and slithered over to me, placing his hands firmly on both breasts.

"They are everything I imagined they would be. You're so perfect, baby. So fucking perfect that I could come in my pants just staring at your beautiful naked body." His fingers faintly traced the outline of my breasts before he bent down and took my excited nipple between his lips. The rise in heat between my thighs was overpowering as the excitement dripped from me. His tongue licked around one hardened nipple while his hand kneaded and groped my other breast. He was giving equal attention to both, and my body appreciated it. He took my hand and led me over to the bed.

"I want you to lie on your stomach."

I did just that as he hovered over me, his tongue making tiny circles up and down my backside and his erection pressing firmly between my legs. I wanted him inside me, and I wanted him now. I felt like I couldn't take anymore.

"Simon, please fuck me," I begged.

"In due time," he whispered in between small, erotic kisses. "First, you're going to come for me like you did earlier. We have all night to play, and we're going to take full advantage of it."

He turned me around so I was now on my back and stood up in front of the bed, unzipping his pants and sliding them off his hips. My lips began to quiver as he took down his underwear and released his large, throbbing cock. The thickness and length of him frightened me. He was twice the size of Brendon. He smiled at me when he caught me staring at his goods.

"Do you like what you see?" he asked slyly.

"Yes," I gulped.

He hooked his fingers into the sides of my panties and slid them down my legs, taking them off and bringing the crotch up to his nose. "Your smell drives me insane, Gabrielle." He tossed them to the side and bent down, pushing my legs apart and burying his face in between my thighs. His tongue licked up and down my wet opening and then made tiny circles around my swollen, aching clit. I threw my head back as my legs tightened like force grips around his head. Before I knew it, his fingers dipped inside me. I thrust up my hips with the sweet rhythm of his movements, and light moans escaped my lips.

"That's right, baby, enjoy it." His tongue lightly brushed over my clit as the intensity of my uprising orgasm grew. My hands fell to my sides as I gripped the bed sheets as hard as I could, and my body lost all control. "That was amazing." Simon smiled as he ran his tongue across his lips and hovered over me, smashing his mouth against mine and tangling his fingers in my hair.

"I'm losing control, Gabrielle, and I need to be inside you. I need to fuck you right now."

As I tried to control my breathing, I nodded. There was a desperation in his voice that I'd never heard before.

"Are you on any birth control?"

"Yes, but you've been with too many women, Simon."

"I'm clean, and I need you to trust me. I can prove it to you after I fuck you. Trust me, Gabrielle. Do you trust me?"

"Yes," I whispered. Simon Young wasn't the type of man who would let himself contract an STD. At least, I hoped not.

His mouth found its way to my breasts, nipping at my erect nipple with his teeth and tugging the other with his fingers. "Stroke my cock before I put it inside you. I want to feel your soft, beautiful hand around it."

I reached over and placed my hand around his thickness, stroking him slowly up and down. Feral groans rumbled up his throat as he threw his head back and closed his eyes. After a few pumps, he removed my hand, grabbed the other, and held both of my hands above my head while he grabbed ahold of his cock and placed it at the edge of my opening. His pacific blue eyes danced with excitement as he stared into mine, and he gently pushed himself into me. I gasped. He gasped.

"Fuck, baby. You're so tight," he moaned as he pushed deeper into me.

My body was on fire, and I'd never felt anything like it. His cock gave me such a different feeling inside than Brendon's ever did.

"Oh my God, you feel so good," he voiced with bated breath.

He stopped and rolled me with him so I was on top. "Sit all the way up and let me watch those beautiful tits bounce up and down as you grind my cock."

As I sat up, he gripped my hips and pushed me down. He was so deep inside me that I thought I was going to explode. Once I began moving back and forth, his hands reached up and grabbed my breasts as he squeezed them in an erotic way.

"You are so fucking beautiful, baby. Everything about you is beautiful. Ride me, Gabrielle. Ride me fast and hard."

His words excited me, and I couldn't hold back. Just knowing how excited and turned on he was by me gave me the confidence and strength to please him. He licked his thumb and placed it on my clit, rubbing it around in circles as I rode him. I couldn't stop the loud moans that came from deep inside me.

"That's right, baby. Tell me how I make you feel."

"Amazing," I let out breathlessly.

"I need you to stop," he said as he placed his hands on my hips. "I was about to come and don't want to come just yet."

He kissed me as I climbed off of him, and he sat up. "Get back on." He smiled as he held his rock-hard cock in his hand.

I bit down on my bottom lip as I placed my legs on each side of him and slowly sat on him, taking in his entire length. He wrapped his arms around me tightly as I moved back and forth, hitting the right spot for both of us.

"Ah, that's it. If you can hold out, I want you to come with me. Just a few more strokes, baby."

This was it. My body was ready to release another orgasm, and I wanted to scream with pleasure, but I had to remember where we were. Simon's moans grew louder as he held me down and filled my insides with his come. We sat there, holding each other tight. This day, this moment was unlike anything I'd ever experienced before. Simon looked at me and held my face in his hands, softly kissing my lips.

"I hope you enjoyed that." He smiled.

I couldn't help but let out a light laugh. "Of course I did. I hope I didn't disappoint you."

He tilted his head as he pushed my hair behind my ear. "You were amazing." He pulled me into a warm embrace.

Chapter Seventeen

"Would you like to go to the restaurant and eat dinner, or would you prefer to order room service?" he asked as he buttoned up his shirt. "I was thinking you could buy since you scammed my casino." He winked.

"Very funny." I smiled. "How about we just stay in and order room service for tonight? I'm a little tired."

"That's something I don't want to hear." He stepped closer to me and kissed my lips. "I'm not even finished with you yet."

"Don't tease me," I moaned as I kissed him back.

"Oh, darling, I don't tease. If you think for one second I'm done with that sexy body of yours, you're crazy." He took the room service menu from the desk.

"This is your hotel. You don't know what they serve?"

"You're cocky. I like you." He winked.

"I like you too. I think I'm going to take a bath. Just order me whatever you're having."

"Okay. There are bathrobes in the closet, but I would prefer if you walked around the suite naked."

His tone was serious. There wasn't even a hint of joking in his voice. I shut the door and started the bath. As I climbed into the hot and bubbly water, I couldn't stop thinking about this amazing day and how Simon made me feel so comfortable. Shit. Who was I kidding? I felt unleashed like a whole new world had opened up for me. My body still tingled from the multiple orgasms of the day. I needed to shut down my brain and push all my emotions to the back of my mind. There could be no attachment. As long as he wanted my body, he could have it. No strings. We both reaped the benefits and, as he said, no complications. He lightly tapped on the door and peeked his head inside.

"Your friend, Giana, just called. I took the liberty of answering it for you. I told her you were in the bath and that you'd call her when you got out."

"Oh, okay. Thanks." I smiled.

"By the way, she asked if we had fucked yet, and I told her yes. I hope you don't mind." He winked and shut the door.

Leave it to G to be bold and ask questions like that. After stepping out of the tub, I dried off and put on the white bathrobe I took from the closet. When I walked back into the main area of the suite, our dinner had just arrived.

"Perfect timing. Dinner is served."

"I can see that. What did you end up ordering?"

"Sit down and find out." He pulled out the chair for me.

I lifted the lid from the plate, and there sat a beautiful steak, a nice-sized lobster tail, and a baked sweet potato.

"I hope you like steak and lobster."

"I do. Thank you. It looks delicious. You need to change the color of the robes in your new hotel."

"Huh?" he asked in confusion.

The Secret He Holds

"White is so standard, and every hotel in the world has them. Be different and be diverse. Don't you want to be known as the hotel that has the colored robes?"

"And what color would you suggest?"

"Black for the men and pink for the women."

He raised his eyebrow as he cut into his steak. "I like it. Good idea. If you want to do it, then let's do it."

"Really?" I asked with surprise.

"Why not? I never gave robe colors much thought, but if you think it'll be a hit, let's do it." He smiled.

We finished our dinner, and Simon poured me another glass of wine. He stood in front of me and took the strings of my robe in his hands. "I thought I told you that I wanted you to walk around naked."

"I'm cold."

"Oh, baby, I can warm that body up real fast." He grinned as he untied it and pushed it off my shoulders, leaning in and kissing me. He took my hand and looked at my arm.

Fuck! I forgot about my scar. Fear crept up inside me as he looked into my eyes. "What happened to your arm? Why didn't I notice that before?"

"It was an accident I had long ago," I replied nervously. I reached down, grabbed the robe from the floor, and slipped it back on.

"What kind of accident?" he demanded to know. "And how have you been keeping it covered up?"

"I don't want to talk about it," I snapped as I turned away from him. "I have a special makeup that covers scars."

"Don't turn away from me, Gabrielle. Tell me what kind of accident it was."

"Damn it, Simon. No."

I was scared. What would he think of me?

"Do you remember me telling you that I don't take no for an answer? Now, tell me."

"Fine. You really want to fucking know?!" I screamed at him. "I used to cut."

The look on his face turned from anger to complete horror.

"If you look closely at my arms, you can still see the marks. I needed to stop the emotional pain. My childhood, my life, Brendon. One day, Brendon and I got into a fight, and he said some horrible things to me. Things I couldn't stand to hear anymore. He stormed out of the penthouse, and I took a razor blade, and I slipped. I cut too deep." Tears filled my eyes. "Now you know, so think whatever you want to think, but you've never walked in my shoes."

I placed my hands on the chair that was in front of me, and I felt Simon's strong arms wrap around me.

"Oh, Gabrielle. I'm sorry. Please don't cry, baby." He kissed the back of my head before turning me around and holding me tight. "It's okay."

Picking me up and carrying me to the bedroom, he gently laid me on the bed and climbed next to me, wrapping me up in his arms as if he were protecting me.

"That was the last time I ever cut," I whispered.

"I'm glad to hear that." He kissed my head.

~

It was two a.m. when I opened my eyes and looked at the clock. Simon was rolled over on his other side as I quietly got out of bed and went to the refrigerator for a bottle of water. I lifted up the sleeve of my robe and looked at the scar on my arm.

"Is everything okay?" I heard Simon's voice say.

"Yeah. I was just thirsty. I didn't mean to wake you."

He walked over to me, took my arm, and brought it up to his lips, kissing my scar.

"It's okay. You don't need to be ashamed of it. It was an accident. Come back to bed, and I promise to make you feel better." He smiled as his lips touched mine.

I nodded my head, and he swooped down and picked me up.

Before I knew it, the alarm went off. Simon moaned as he reached over and turned it off. I was snuggled against his body and fell asleep with my head on his chest. He had given me two more orgasms before going to sleep. He sent me into dreamland, and I was scared that all of this was only a dream.

"We need to get up and get ready for the meeting." He kissed the top of my head.

"I'm nervous, Simon."

"There's no need to be nervous. Let's go take a shower."

I held the sheet over my naked body as he climbed out of bed. He was just as sexy in the morning; his hair was slightly messed up, and his face stubble, which had grown more overnight.

"Well, what are you waiting for? Get that sexy ass out of bed and join me in the shower."

Stepping in first, Simon held out his hand to me. After I stepped in next to him, he reached over and slid the glass door shut. His hands massaged my breasts as his lips tended to my neck. I reached down and took his thick manhood in my hand. He moaned as the hot water streamed down our bodies and my hand slowly but firmly moved up and down his shaft. He threw his head back as feral sounds escaped his lips. It was my turn to pleasure him in the best way possible. My tongue slowly moved across his chest and down his torso, dipping into every crevice of his masculine six-pack. I didn't think he could get any harder than he already was, but I was wrong. I continued my journey down his happy trail, licking and softly kissing until I reached his manhood. Slowly taking him in my mouth, he sharply inhaled as his fingers fisted my hair. As I moved my mouth up and down his length, he began to thrust his hips.

"Good God, Gabrielle, you're—Oh my God," he moaned as my tongue swirled around his engorged head and I softly stroked his balls. He gave his hips one last thrust and grunted as he filled my mouth with pleasure. "I was not expecting that." He smiled as he kissed me.

"Did you enjoy it?" I uttered as his fingers plunged inside me.

"I've never enjoyed something so much in my life. I thought you were inexperienced?"

I tried to steady myself as he worked his fingers around my insides. "I am," I said with bated breath.

"Like hell you are, baby." His mouth smashed into mine as he placed his thumb on my already swollen clit, pressing down and rubbing in tiny circles. "Now it's your turn."

Breaking our kiss and coming up for air, I placed my mouth on his shoulder, nipping at his skin as I was about to come. My knees became weak as I shuddered, and my body gave in to his pleasuring touch. He smiled at me and kissed my lips.

"We really need to get moving with this shower. We're going to be late if we keep this up."

"I know. But I didn't expect you to give me a morning blowjob. You've set my body on fire, Gabrielle, and I don't know if I can stop." His smile enticed me.

"Down, boy. What will your boys in the meeting think

if we walk in together late? Rumors would start." I laughed as I reached for the shampoo.

We were able to finish our shower without any more pleasurable fondling, and we both got ready and headed down to the conference room.

Chapter Eighteen

"You were amazing," Simon chimed as he held up his glass.

"Thank you. It felt amazing." I smiled as I held up mine.

As I dipped into my grilled chicken salad, Simon's phone rang. The bright, cheery face that had stared at me all morning turned somber.

"I'll be there in a few hours." He hung up.

"What's wrong?"

"We have to leave. My grandfather has taken a turn for the worse, and he doesn't have much time left. I need to get back to Seattle."

"Of course."

We pushed our plates to the side and got up from the table. As we walked to the elevator, Simon called his pilot and told him we needed to leave right away. When we got back to the room, I quickly gathered my things and repacked my suitcase. Simon was silent. It was almost as if he completely shut down. I tried to talk to him, but he just gave one-word answers. The bellhop came and collected our bags as we climbed into the limousine that was waiting for us outside the hotel. I pulled out my phone and sent G a text message.

"Flying home today. Simon's grandfather took a turn for the worse."

"Oh no. That's terrible. Glad you're coming home. I can't wait to hear all about your fucktacious adventures!"

"See you in a few hours."

I looked over at Simon and caught him staring at me and then at my phone. "G." I smiled.

He gave a small smile, turned away, and looked out the window. I could see the sadness that resided in his eyes, and I wanted to comfort him. I slowly reached out my hand and placed it on top of him. He pulled away. Maybe he needed space. Time to let it soak in that this was it. That his grandfather would be gone forever. I didn't say a word. When he was ready to talk, he'd let me know.

I spent my time thinking as we sat on the plane while Simon sat on his laptop. As hard as I tried to push my emotions to the side, I couldn't. The last couple of days we spent together were the best days of my life and ones that wouldn't be so easily forgotten. I looked over at him as he worked. His face was so tender and sad. I hated that he wouldn't talk to me about what he was feeling. I didn't care anymore. I wanted to wrap my arms around him and comfort him. I got up from my seat and walked over to the couch where he was sitting. I sat down next to him, and he looked at me. I placed my hand on his cheek and stared into his sad eyes. He didn't turn away as he fixated his gaze on me. Suddenly, his mouth crashed into mine before he stood up and carried me to his bed on the plane. He needed this, his control. He couldn't control his grandfather's life, which was hanging by a thread, but he could control me, and at that moment, I let him. He wasted no time pulling down my pants and flipping me over to take me from behind. His carnal movements excited me physically, but emotionally, I was hurting. As he thrust hard into me one last time, he released himself inside of me, gripping my ass so tight I was sure he left marks. When he finished, he pulled out of me and walked out of the room. I lay there as tears sprang to my eyes.

After collecting myself and putting my pants back on, I opened the door and walked back to my seat. Simon was sitting in a chair on the right, holding a glass of bourbon while he stared out the window. I took a seat on the left and buckled up, for it was almost time to land. I wouldn't look at him because I couldn't. All he had to do was say one word to me after he fucked me senseless. Even a thank you would have made all the difference in the world.

The plane landed, and Simon exited the plane before I did. All I could think was, "Wow." I grabbed my luggage, stepped off the plane, and headed in the opposite direction of the limousine that was waiting for us on the runway.

"Where are you going?" Simon yelled.

"Anywhere you aren't!" I yelled back. I wasn't playing this clusterfuck of a game with him. Now I was pissed as hell.

"Get back here!"

I heard his footsteps approaching me as I tried to walk as fast as I could. I was almost at the airport door. It wasn't much further. He caught up with me and stood in front of me. I halted.

"The limo is the other way. I don't have time for this. Turn around, and please get in the limo."

I looked him straight in the eyes as I said deadpan, "NO! I'm going to take a cab."

"I'm sorry, Gabrielle. Please," he begged.

There was a sincerity in his voice. I looked down and then all around.

"Please."

I didn't say anything. I turned around, and he took my bag from me as we headed to the limo. The ride to my apartment was silent. He didn't try to talk to me again, and I didn't try to talk to him. Patrick pulled up to the curb, got out, opened my door, and then took my bag from the back. I couldn't leave without saying something to Simon. Obviously, he wasn't going to say a word by how he looked at me.

"Thanks" was the word that I could barely mutter.

As I got out of the limo, he grabbed my hand. I turned my head and saw the sadness that consumed his eyes. A moment, a split second passed, but it seemed like forever. He didn't speak. He let go of my hand, and I walked away.

⁓

I inserted the key into the door, and as soon as I opened it, G came running from the kitchen.

"Yay. You're home! I can't wait to hear all about Simon Young. Oh my God, was he fucking amazing? Did he spoil you? Tell me!" she squealed as she grabbed my hand.

"He was something, all right." I gave a small, non-convincing smile.

G frowned and slowly shook her head. "What's wrong? What happened, Gabby?"

"I don't know," I replied with tears in my eyes.

She wrapped her arms around me and gave me a warm hug. After a few moments, she walked to the kitchen, grabbed a bottle of wine and two glasses, and sat on the couch beside me. I told her about my time with Simon. The things he did, the sex, and his behavior after he got the phone call about his grandfather. But I didn't tell her what happened on the plane. That was probably the first and only thing I'd never told her.

"Gabby, what did I tell you about letting your emotions get in the way? Physically, Simon made you feel amazing, and that's all you need. You just got out of a bad relationship and don't need to go through this again."

"I know. But—"

"No buts. Simon Young isn't a man you can trust. He's a millionaire playboy who loves to hook up with different women. Not just one woman. I don't mean to hurt you, but the man will never commit to one girl. He even told you that. You've been hurt enough for the past six years, and I couldn't stand to see you go through that again."

"You're right." I laid my head on her shoulder. "He's just so fucking amazing in bed."

"And that's all you need. If he keeps wanting to have sex with you, then great. If that's all he wants, even better. You don't need this complication in your life. Have sex, have fun. You only live once, Gabs. It's time you start."

～

Six a.m., and I was already up on a Saturday morning. Grabbing my phone from the nightstand, I checked to see if I had any messages. Zero. Why did I expect that Simon would text me? Everything G said to me last night was true. I didn't need any complications in my life. I was starting fresh and building a new life for myself. My main focus had to be my job, and the rest would eventually fall into place. Fuck him. That was my new motto.

I stumbled into the kitchen to make some coffee. I jumped when I saw Donovan sitting at the table.

"You scared me. When did you get here?"

"Sorry, Gabby. I came over late last night. You were already sleeping."

"And why are you up so early?" I asked as I poured a cup of coffee.

"Couldn't sleep. You're welcome for the coffee." He smiled.

"Thanks." I held up my cup.

This was awkward. I wasn't fond of Donovan because of what he was doing. If he weren't a cheating bastard, he'd be a great guy.

"Sorry your trip got cut short."

"Yeah. Shit happens. It's nice to be back home. Muffin?" I asked.

"Nah. I'm good."

"So your wife comes back tomorrow, eh?"

"Yep. She sure does." He sighed.

I sat at the table and nodded my head. Just as I was about to say something, G strolled into the kitchen and wrapped her arms around Donovan's neck.

"I woke up so lonely," she whined.

"Sorry, baby girl, I couldn't sleep, and I didn't want to wake you."

"Hello. Good morning." I waved.

"Good morning. Did you sleep well?"

"Obviously, I did since I didn't even hear Donovan come over."

"That's great. You needed the rest." She poured herself a cup of coffee.

"You two enjoy your morning. I'm going out for a run."

"Really?" G asked with a surprised tone.

"Yes. I haven't worked out since I got here, and now it's time for me to get back into it and a routine."

"Have fun and go run down by the waterfront. It's pretty."

I walked to the bedroom and changed into a pair of cropped yoga pants and a T-shirt. After throwing my hair up in a ponytail and brushing my teeth, I put on my running shoes and stepped outside to the overcast grey sky. It looked like it might rain, but I didn't care. I still ran the two miles to the waterfront. Because it was still early, there weren't many people around, and it was nice. G was right; it was pretty here, especially in the early morning. I turned up the volume on my iPod to try to drown out all thoughts of Simon. Thoughts I no longer wanted to consume my mind. After running about three miles, I noticed my shoe was untied, so I stopped to tie it. As I was bent down, tying my shoe, I noticed a pair of legs in grey sweatpants and Nike shoes standing in front of me. I slowly looked up, and my heart stopped as he held out his hand.

"I didn't expect to see you here."

"Well, I didn't expect to see you here either," I replied.

He gave me a small smile, but something in his eyes seemed sad.

"How's your grandfather?"

"He's as well as can be expected, I guess."

An awkward silence had set in, and I still didn't understand it after everything we'd done. He looked so sexy in his sweatpants and white Nike t-shirt. Fuck, this man looked sexy in anything he wore and nothing. The Simon ache was back, and I wanted to die. My body was craving him, and I needed to get out of his sight.

"I have to go. I'll see you Monday at the office." Before I could jog away, he reached out and lightly took hold of my arm.

"Please, don't go just yet."

When I turned and looked at him, his eyes pleaded with me, sending my strong will out the window.

"I should."

"You shouldn't. Come back to my house with me." His eyes never left mine.

"Simon, yesterday—"

"Fuck yesterday. Gabrielle, I want to see you. Please."

I took my bottom lip between my teeth, and I could have told him a thousand reasons why it wasn't a good idea. But I missed him, and the thought of going to his house and spending some time with him overruled.

"Fine. I have to go home, shower, and change first."

"Then let's do dinner. I'll have Patrick pick you up around five o'clock, and I'll have my chef cook us something really nice."

"Okay. I'll be ready. Now, if you'll excuse me, I better get going."

He nodded. "Okay. I'll see you later," he said with a small smile as he ran the back of his hand down my cheek.

Fuck, my panties were already soaked just from seeing him and our conversation. I knew damn well what was going to happen tonight, and my body screamed with excitement. As soon as I opened the door to the apartment, I heard moans coming from G's room.

"I'm back!" I yelled across the apartment.

"Okay," Donovan yelled back.

I rolled my eyes and jumped into the shower to wash off the sweat from my run and to make sure I was more than freshened up for tonight.

Chapter Nineteen

I slid into the back of the limo in my strappy blue baby doll dress with a cut-out back and a pair of black-heeled ankle boots.

"Thank you for picking me up, Patrick."

"My pleasure, Gabrielle."

"Where does Simon actually live?"

"His house is in Medina."

"Oh. Very nice. But I wouldn't expect anything less from him." I smiled.

Patrick pulled up to the large wrought-iron gates and punched in the code. As the gates slowly opened, my stomach started to flutter, not only at the thought of seeing Simon but the sight of his monstrous house.

"Wow. Look at this place."

I heard Patrick chuckle. "It's a beauty. That's for sure."

He pulled up the long, winding drive and stopped in front of the house. Big, beautiful trees lined the front and around the sides, giving the property the privacy it deserved. Patrick opened the door for me and helped me out.

"Have a nice night, Gabrielle." He smiled.

"Thank you. I intend to."

Before I stepped up the many multiple-stone stairs to the porch, the front door opened, and Simon stood there in a pleasing manner that sent the Simon ache right down to my toes.

"You look amazing." He smiled as he took my hand and brought it up to his lips.

"Thank you. So do you."

"Welcome to my home, Gabrielle."

As soon as I stepped through the large double doors with the floral glass design, I was in awe of the oak flooring and Parisian taupe walls that complemented each other well. He led me into the library and shut the door. One side of the wall was lined with beautiful oak bookcases, the other had a gas fireplace, and the other had a row of windows overlooking the lake.

"This is beautiful, Simon. It seems very peaceful," I spoke as I stared out the window.

"It is," he responded, wrapping his arms around my waist from behind.

My skin started to heat up from his touch, and my heart began to beat a little faster.

"Have I told you how beautiful and sexy you look?" The warmth of his breath grazed my neck.

"Yes, but please keep telling me." I laughed.

His lips lightly pressed against my skin as his hands moved up the back of my dress, firmly gripping my ass. My lips parted as a delicate moan escaped them.

"You love it when I squeeze your perfect ass, don't you? I want to hear you say it." I could feel his erection against my back.

"Yes," I whispered as he tightened his grip.

"Yes, what, Gabrielle?" His tongue glided down my ear.

"I love it."

"I need to see if you're telling me the truth," his soft voice spoke.

He moved the cotton crotch of my panties to the side and plunged his finger inside, feeling the excitement of what he'd done to me. "Damn, you're so wet already. You do love it, don't you, baby?"

"Yes," I replied with bated breath as he inserted another finger.

"Do you want to come, Gabrielle?" His fingers manipulated my insides, and his tongue made soft circles around my shoulder.

"Yes, please."

He removed his fingers and turned me around so I was facing him. He got down on his knees and hooked his thumbs into the sides of my panties, pulling them down and lifting my foot so he could remove them. I knew what was coming, and my body screamed in excitement. That mouth of his was talented, and he knew how to use it. His hands traveled up my legs and under my dress until his hands gripped my hips. Sliding his tongue between my legs and up until he reached my already sensitive area, and with the flick of his tongue on my clit, he sent me into euphoria. Low moans rumbled in his throat as he licked and bathed his mouth in my pleasurable juices. His hands tightened on my hips as I thrust into him, throwing my head back as I was ready to climax.

"Don't stop," I begged.

As he embedded his finger inside of me and stroked my swollen clit with his tongue, my body shuddered as I placed my hand over my mouth to shield the noises that were about to come from me. My heart rate quickened as the gratifying climax happened, leaving me to grip his shoulders for support as my legs steadily shook. Simon stood up and cupped the back of my neck as his wet mouth crashed into mine, devouring me, leaving little room for breath.

"It's time for dinner." He smiled as he bent down and pulled up my panties, taking my hand and leading me out of the library.

Simon pulled out the chair for me, and I sat down at the elegant table that was fitted for eight people. A man in a chef's uniform approached and set down a plate in front of me. A plate that consisted of some kind of chicken in a cream sauce, fresh green beans, roasted potatoes, and a side salad with raspberry vinaigrette dressing.

"This looks and smells delicious." I lay my napkin in my lap.

"I'm sure you need a drink now after that." Simon winked as he poured me a glass of wine.

My cheeks heated because I knew that wasn't the end of it for the night. I was sure he had many other things for us planned sexually, and I was getting excited just thinking about it. Thoughts of other women crept into my mind. Did he do this sort of thing with all the women he'd been with? Of course, he did, and I would be stupid to think otherwise. We ate dinner and discussed Young International and his new hotel plans. After we finished, Simon took me outside to the back to view his property. It was simply breathtaking. Pavers made up the enormously large patio with a breathtaking infinity pool in the middle, surrounded by in-ground lights and potted plants. Patio furniture was scattered around, ranging from fancy lounge chairs to small bistro sets. Looking over the large trees and beautifully sculpted shrubbery was Lake Washington, the property's focal point.

"This is simply beautiful. I'll be honest with you," I said as I turned and looked at him, "I would have expected a much bigger house from you."

"You don't think seven thousand square feet is big enough?" He smirked.

"I do. But...I don't know. I pegged your house to be one of those you walk into, and it looks like a museum."

He laughed. "I like comfort and peace. This house is very peaceful and comfortable. I also want my guests to feel comfortable and not like they're not allowed to touch anything."

"I like it."

Simon walked over to the outdoor bar and poured me another glass of wine. "Another?"

"Thank you."

We took seats in the two cushiony lounge chairs that faced the pool. I set my glass down and crossed my arms, rubbing them to take away the chill.

"Are you cold?"

"A little."

He got up from the chair and went inside the house. A few moments later, he returned, placed a navy blue zip-up hoodie around my shoulders, then bent down and brushed his lips against mine.

"Thank you."

"You're welcome. The last thing I want is for you to be cold."

Chapter Twenty

I wanted to talk to him about yesterday. How his attitude had changed and his actions on the plane. He just couldn't behave that way if we were going to be friends.

"We need to talk about yesterday," I nervously spoke.

"I already apologized for yesterday."

"You just can't do a complete switch like that. It's not fair."

"Gabrielle," he spoke in a serious tone. "I do what I want and can behave however I want."

"Even if it hurts the other person?"

"I didn't hurt you. Did I?"

"Physically, no."

"Then you enjoyed when I fucked you on the plane?"

"Well, yes. I mean, no. Well, sort of. You just left me there and walked out. What the fuck was that?"

"Sometimes, that's how I am."

I couldn't respond because I didn't know what to say. On one hand, it bothered me, but on the other, he turned me on like no other man ever had. The way he was always in control excited me. It was a different kind of control than how Brendon was. Brendon was a mere boy trying to fit into the world of being a man. Simon was a man. He was a full-fledged, sexy-as-fuck, controlling man who was always used to getting what he desired. He reached over and held out his hand to me.

"I would like you to spend the night," he said as he softly stroked my hand with his thumb. "You can call Giana and have her pack you a small bag, and I'll have Patrick pick it up."

"Why?"

"Why what? Why do I want you to spend the night?"

"Yes."

His eyes observed me from across the chair. "I want you to spend the night because I want to fuck you all night long and all day tomorrow. I want to wrap my arms around your soft, silky skin, and I want to smell the lavender scent that graces your body as I fall asleep."

Shit. Total panty soaker right there. How does one respond to that?

"Okay," I gulped.

"Okay? That's it?"

"Okay, master?"

He chuckled. "That's good enough for me."

"I have one condition," I bravely spoke.

His left eyebrow arched as he looked at me. "You have a condition? Enlighten me."

"I want you to tell me more about your life. I want to know you better."

He sighed and took a drink from his glass as he stared out at the lake. His smoldering eyes turned and looked at me. "Fine. If that's your condition."

I smiled as I pulled out my phone and sent a text message to G.

"I need you to pack a light bag for me. A couple of outfits, makeup, a bra, and lots of panties. I have a feeling I may be needing them."

"You're staying the night with him? No emotions, right? Just great sex?"

"Yep. No emotions. My body is craving his, so...yeah. Patrick will pick up the bag soon. Thank you, G."

"No problem, Gabs. Have fun and be safe."

I couldn't tell her my emotions were at an all-time high. The fact that he wanted me to stay the night with him at his house had to mean a little something. Right? Or was I being delusional, and this was something he frequently did with all his women?

"Giana is packing my bag now."

"Did you tell her to be sure and pack plenty of panties?" He grinned as he pulled out his phone and dialed Patrick.

"Yes, I told her."

"Good."

"Now spill it, Young. I want to know about you."

He got up from his seat and held out his hand to me. "Let's go inside. It's a bit chilly out here. We can sit next to the fire."

I placed my hand in his, and we went to the living room. He turned on the fireplace and then took a seat next to me on the sofa and turned so he was facing me.

"My parents were killed in a train accident in London when I was five years old. They were my only family there, so I was sent back to the States to live with my grandfather. He raised me like his son. He drilled into my head that money and success were everything that life was supposed to be made up of, and he told me every day that Young International, one of the world's largest luxury hotel chains, would be all mine someday. According to him, my father was a failure and didn't see things the way he did. My mom got pregnant with me before she and my dad were married. One night, he packed up all his things, and the two of them moved to London. Apparently, he thought that was far enough to escape my grandfather's wrath. They married and made a home for us there."

"So you had never met your grandfather prior to coming to live with him?"

"No. I had never met the man before that. Imagine how scared I was."

"What about your mom's family?"

"I don't even know if there is any. My grandfather was and still is a very powerful man. He made sure that I was to live with him."

"He never dated or married?"

"He always dated different women, but he would never marry again. His views were pretty much the same as mine."

"Or perhaps you got your views from him?" I asked.

"I've seen enough in my life to form my own views."

"Don't you think life is about more than just money and success?"

"Yes. It's about money, success, and sex with beautiful women." He winked.

I felt a sickness in the pit of my stomach. I didn't know if I wanted to hear any more.

"You are truly beautiful, Gabrielle." He placed his hand on my face and looked deep into my eyes.

There was still a sadness in them that I couldn't explain. This was all about sex and nothing else. I had to keep reminding myself of that. *Don't get too involved, Gabby.* If I did, I'd be torn apart worse than ever.

He took his finger and slid it down my arm, stopping at the scar that he already knew about. Lightly rubbing it, he picked up my arm and pressed his lips against it. The Simon ache was back and begging to be fulfilled.

"Was that enough information for you?" he asked seductively.

"Yes," I replied as he had me hypnotized.

"Good. Then it's time to show you my bedroom."

"I would like that."

We both stood up, and he bent down and picked me up. As I placed my arms around his neck, I smiled. "I can walk, you know."

"I'm fully aware of that, but I'd like to carry you."

He stepped inside the room and put me down. After closing the door and locking it, Simon turned to me, and his eyes looked me up and down as his tongue glided along his lips.

"I need to talk to you first about a couple of things."

He had me nervous. "What?"

He placed his hand on my cheek. God, I just about died every time he did that. "Are you opposed to trying different things?"

"What kind of things?" I gulped.

"Sexual things?"

"If you're talking about anal, I'll stop you right there!" I put my hand up.

"No, not yet, anyway." He snickered. He walked over to the armoire that was sitting in the corner and opened the double doors. After pulling out a pair of handcuffs and a blindfold, he held them up to me.

"Oh," I replied as I stared at them and instantly felt like I was going to throw up.

He walked over to me and set the handcuffs in my hands. "Feel the material. They're soft and I promise they won't hurt you. Okay?"

I nodded. He placed the cuffs on my wrists and tightened them. "How do they feel? Are they too tight?"

"No." I swallowed hard. My heart was racing a mile a minute and my skin became very heated.

Simon kissed the tip of my nose as he took down the spaghetti straps of my dress, letting it fall to my feet.

"I'd been staring at your hard nipples all night through that dress. Thank you for not wearing a bra." His finger traced along my jawline. Once again, he hooked his thumbs in the sides of my panties and took them down.

"Step out," he commanded.

As I stood in front of him completely naked, his hands firmly planted themselves on my breasts.

"You have amazing tits, Gabrielle, and I'm going to enjoy pleasing them fully."

The vibrations down below were already on fire, and we hadn't even started.

"Go lie down on my bed."

I did as he asked, and he placed my arms above my head. He lifted his shirt off, unbuttoned his pants, and slid them off his hips while his eyes never left mine.

"I'm going to blindfold you now. Okay?"

I nodded my head because I couldn't form any words.

"I promise, baby, you have nothing to be nervous about. You're going to love this." He smiled as he placed the blindfold over my eyes. "I'll be right back. I'm going to get something."

Oh fuck. Now, what was he up to, and why did he have to wait until after I was blindfolded to say that?

I heard his footsteps enter the room, and the door clicked shut. I swallowed hard but couldn't resist asking one question.

"Did you go out there naked?"

He chuckled. "Yes. The staff is gone, and there's no one else here but us. Are you comfortable?"

"I guess, considering I've never been handcuffed or blindfolded before."

"Good." I heard a clicking sound, and I tensed.

"What is that?" I nervously asked.

"Relax, baby. It's only a lighter. I'm lighting some candles."

"Umm…you're not doing anything with those candles, are you?"

"No." He laughed. "I'm just setting the ambiance. That's all. I promise."

As I lay there completely naked, wrists tied, and a blindfold covering my eyes, I couldn't help but wonder why he couldn't blindfold me after he lit all the candles. I felt him climb on the bed and the heat of his breath dangerously close to my lips.

"You are so fucking sexy. I can barely control myself," he whispered as his tongue licked my lips.

I felt the light brush of his fingers sweep across my breasts and circle around my nipples. "I've never wanted anyone as much as I want you, Gabrielle."

My breath hitched as my Simon ache was beginning to become unbearable. I wanted to reach out and touch him so badly, but I couldn't. This was part of his plan. He didn't want me touching him until he was done with me. I heard him pick up something, and it sounded like ice. You know, the sound ice in a glass makes when you shake it? My body tensed, and he could tell.

"Relax, baby. We're going to play a little game where I'm going to build your anticipation and heighten your excitement. If you don't like it, I want you to tell me to stop, but before you do, give it a chance because I promise you it'll be the best thing you've ever felt."

I nodded my head. A coldness swept across my lips as he lightly rubbed the ice cube across my mouth. Shivers radiated throughout my body. His tongue slid across my collarbone, up my neck, and to the tip of my earlobe. Small, erotic noises escaped my lips as my sexual arousal heightened. I felt the coldness of the ice cube slide down the center of my breasts and around my erect nipples. After he stimulated one nipple with the ice, he gently sucked it with his warm tongue while circling my other nipple. I threw my head back, and my body tensed.

"Watching you react to the way I'm stimulating your body is giving me more excitement than I ever imagined," his low voice spoke. "Are you enjoying it? Just nod if you are."

I nodded. Suddenly, I felt the cold trail down my torso and hit my belly button. Desperation set in between my legs, and I needed him there. He was making his way down, and the anticipation was haunting me.

"I want you to spread your legs as wide as you can for me," he voiced.

I did as he asked and felt the tingle of the ice cube going up my thigh. I gasped as I tried to control my body. The erotic moans that were escaping my lips grew more intense.

"It's all about control, Gabrielle. Stay in control."

I was already sensitive there, and now he expected me to stay in control. As soon as the cold hit me, I tried to squirm. It was too much. The cold, the feeling, the overall excitement. His hand pressed down on my thigh to keep me from moving. I could tell by his breathing that he was excited. Now, I felt his hand down there with the ice cube as he lightly slid it around my entire pussy. I needed a release between his force on my legs and the ice. My body begged for it, and he knew it. Suddenly, the ice disappeared, and his tongue worked my clit, and I couldn't take it anymore. Cold fingers plunged inside me as the warmth of his tongue caused me to lose all control.

"Now, baby. You can come now. Give it to me. Give me everything you've got."

My body went into a frenzy. I screamed his name as he sent me into oblivion like I'd never been before. The wave of my climax hit me as my body tightened and shook with pure pleasure. I felt his smile against me as his tongue softened.

"Beautiful, Gabrielle. Just beautiful," he whispered as his tongue glided up my torso while his hands firmly grasped my breasts.

He removed the blindfold, and when my eyes met his, he was staring down at me with a smile as he thrust into me with force, moving in and out of me vigorously for a few moments.

"God, you feel so good, baby. I could stay inside your warm, delicious pussy all night." His hot breath swept across my back, and his hands worked my breasts. My wrists were still bound and ached to touch him as another orgasm brewed up inside. His thrusts became faster and harder, and his moans grew more intense, sending me over the edge again.

"Ah, I feel you coming, and it's amazing." He pushed deep inside me as he released himself, slowing his movement and filling my insides with his come.

We lay there as our breathing slowly returned to normal, and our heart rates slowed down. His mouth gently kissed my shoulder and up the side of my neck. He let go of me as he undid the cuffs and threw them on the floor. I curled up into him, snuggling my head into his firm and muscular chest. I was exhausted and had never felt so good.

Chapter Twenty-One

My hand lightly brushed over the thin fabric of the sheet that was covering his morning erection, and I lay wrapped tightly in his arms. It was a closeness and security that I had craved my entire life. Brendon never cuddled. He didn't like it. After "so-called" sex, he would turn the other way, sometimes – okay, most of the time – without giving me a kiss. Before Simon and I fell asleep last night, he kissed my head, forehead, nose, and lips. The attention this man was giving me was overwhelming, and it scared me. I could feel the emotions rearing their ugly little heads, smiling, and pleading with me to let them out of their prison that was the state of my mind.

"Good morning. Please feel free to touch my cock again. Preferably under the sheet," he spoke in his sexy, gruff morning voice.

I couldn't help but giggle as I stuck my hand under the sheet and stroked his manhood with the tips of my fingers. His grip around me tightened.

"How about a morning blow before I take that hot

body of yours and fuck you in the shower? But give me those lips first before you wrap them around my cock."

I sat up and gave him a smile as our lips locked. His hand cupped the back of my neck, bringing me closer and into a deep and passionate kiss. Once he let go and broke the kiss, I slid down until I reached him and gave him what he asked for.

After our long shower, I stepped out and wrapped a towel around me, taking notice that he had brought my bag up and set it on the bed. After I dressed in my outfit for the day, Simon stepped out of the bathroom with a towel wrapped around his waist.

"How about breakfast? We can cook together," he said as he pulled a pair of underwear from his dresser drawer.

"That sounds great. I'm starving. I'll go down and put on a pot of coffee." I started to walk out of the room.

"Gabrielle?"

"Yeah." I turned around.

"How about some tea instead?" He smiled.

"Tea it is."

I went to the kitchen and over to the largest walk-in refrigerator I had ever seen. It was stocked with fruits, vegetables, meats, cheeses, and everything else you could imagine. I pulled out the carton of eggs and some vegetables to make omelets. As I began chopping the vegetables, Simon walked in.

"Omelets?" he asked.

"If that's okay?"

"I love omelets." He walked to the cabinet and pulled out the box of tea. "What should we do today?"

Without looking at him and instead focusing on the vegetables, I said, "I thought we were going to fuck all day?"

He walked over and placed his hand on my hip,

lowering his mouth to my ear. "We are, but we need to give that pussy of yours and my cock a little bit of a break. Not too long, though, so don't worry." He kissed my ear.

Excitement sprang to my lower half as I clenched my legs together. Simon heated the pan and cracked the eggs. Being in the kitchen with him and cooking together was wonderful. This was the type of relationship I'd always wanted. But I had to remember that this wasn't a "real" relationship. It was still nice.

After we finished breakfast, I helped Simon clean up, and we went and sat outside for a while. It was a beautiful day and a bit warmer than it had previously been.

"I want you to focus solely on the new hotel and nothing else. I'm handing it all over to you, Gabrielle."

"What? That's a lot of responsibility, Simon."

"You can do it, and I know you'll do an amazing job. People around the office will talk. Ignore them. Do you understand me?"

"I guess."

"I want you to handle every detail and aspect. If you run into a problem, you come to me and only me. You will be rewarded for your efforts. This new hotel is yours, and I want you to live and breathe it."

"I'm only the marketing expert, Simon."

"You'll learn the rest. You're intelligent, and if I didn't think you could do it, I wouldn't give you all the responsibility. After all, you ripped off my casino." He winked.

We ended up spending the entire day together. We took a walk down by the lake, made love a couple of times, talked about silly things, and cooked dinner.

"I'm going to drive you home," Simon said as he grabbed his keys.

"I thought Patrick was?" I asked as the excitement of driving with him consumed me.

"I want to. It's the least I could do to thank you for spending the weekend with me. I really enjoyed having you here." His hand cupped the back of my neck as his thumb slowly stroked my cheek.

"Do you do this often with other women?" A jealousy that I didn't know existed came out of hiding.

"I won't answer that question because discussions about other women are off-limits. Do you understand?" he asked in a rigid tone.

I stared at the seriousness in his eyes before I answered. "Yes, I understand."

"Good. Now let's get you home before G starts blowing up your phone, wondering where you are."

I didn't want to leave him. The time we spent together in Vegas and now at his home dominated me. Not only my body but my thoughts as well.

~

When I walked through my apartment door, G wasn't home. I found it odd since Donovan's wife was coming home today, and I thought she'd be here. It was getting late, so I changed into my pajamas and sat down on the couch to watch a movie. The front door opened.

"You're back!" G exclaimed as she sat down next to me. "I want all the juicy, sexy details."

"Where were you? I thought you would have been home since Donovan's wife was coming back today."

"I was out to dinner with Jared. Donovan had to go pick up his bitch wife at the airport. I miss him already, Gabby." She pouted.

I sighed as I put my arm around her. "You're really into him, aren't you?"

She laid her head on my shoulder. "I am in love with him, and he's in love with me."

"Then why hasn't he left his wife yet?"

"He's going to. He's finalizing some paperwork work regarding his properties tomorrow. I can't even believe the feeling I get when I'm with him."

"I know, right?" I slipped.

She lifted her head and looked at me. "What's going on with you and Simon? Just amazing sex, right?"

"Sure. No. I mean, yes, but it's hard. You know? He makes me feel special, like I'm the only woman in the world."

"But you're not. He's a womanizer. I'm sorry to say this, Gabs, but you're his flavor of the month, so to speak. A man like Simon can't commit. You need to convince yourself of that. He's rebuilding everything about you that Dickwad took away. He's giving you confidence, and you're going to need that to move on to the next guy that looks your way."

"Flavor the month, eh?" I smiled. "I'm going to bed." I kissed her head. "A full day of sex really wears a girl out."

"You're awesome, and don't forget that!" she yelled across the apartment as I walked to my room and shut the door.

I heard my phone beep, and when I opened my eyes and looked at the clock, it was three thirty a.m. I grabbed my phone, and there was a text message from Simon.

"My grandfather passed away. I won't be in the office all week. I just wanted you to know."

My heart broke; he needed me. My first instinct was to get dressed and drive over to his house.

"I'm so sorry, Simon. I can come over right now."

"No. Don't. Stay where you're at. I want to be alone."

I was surprised by his response.

"Then I'll see you at the funeral. When is it?"

"Tuesday. But don't bother. It's going to be a private funeral. That's what he wanted. I'll talk to you soon. Have a good week at work."

"Simon, wait."

He didn't respond. My feelings were hurt. He shut me out. After everything we shared this weekend, he still shut me out. Tears sprang to my eyes, and I hated myself for letting them. I hated myself for thinking that I was special to him. I was nothing but another pawn in his game. A game he played frequently and was the master at.

Chapter Twenty-Two

As I walked to my office, Katie jumped up from her desk and fetched me a cup of coffee. I looked at the piles of folders on my desk and sighed as I sat down in my chair.

"Good morning, Gabby. Did you hear?" She handed me a cup of coffee.

"Morning. Hear what?"

"About Mr. Young passing away. Not Simon, of course, but his grandfather."

"Yeah, I heard."

"Are you okay?" she asked with sincerity.

"I'm just tired. I was up all night."

"How was Vegas?"

"It was fine. The meeting went great."

"And? Anything else?"

"Like?" I asked.

"I don't know." She shrugged. "I was just curious if you got to know Mr. Young better."

"No. We're friends and business associates, that's all.

Do me a favor and tell everyone I'm busy today. I don't want to be disturbed unless it's absolutely necessary."

"Okay. If you need anything, let me know." She smiled as she walked out of my office and shut the door.

The hours, the minutes, and the days passed slowly. I spent the week burying myself in my work and missing Simon. I hadn't heard from him since that night, four days ago. The funeral had come and gone, and I thought maybe he'd be back in the office, but he never showed up. I broke down on the day of his grandfather's funeral and sent him a text message to let him know that I was thinking of him. He didn't respond. Not even a thank you. I met with several teams to discuss the hotel project. This was going to be Young International's first hotel that would cater to middle-class people with more affordable rates without cutting the luxury that made the Young name, and it was my job to figure out how to do it.

It was now Friday, and as I looked over some renovation reports, Giana walked into my office, holding a bag.

"Well, look at this fancy office you have. I swear it's better than mine." She smiled as she stood in the doorway.

"Welcome to my home away from home."

"I brought us lunch. You need a break." She set the plastic bag on the desk and took a seat across from me.

"Aren't you supposed to be at work?"

"I took a half day. Donovan is out of town, and I was caught up with my cases, so I thought I'd swing by since I've barely seen you all week."

"I'm buried in work."

"You choose to be buried in work. Any word from Simon yet?"

I shook my head as I took the Styrofoam containers out of the bag. After finishing a nice lunch, Giana left to shop for groceries. She had invited Jared over for dinner tonight and wanted to know if I'd be there. She was pleased when I told her I would.

"Gabby?" Katie poked her head in the door.

I looked up from my computer. "What's up?"

"I just thought you should know that Mr. Young is back in the office today."

The twinge in my stomach revived itself. He was here and didn't bother to let me know.

"Thank you for letting me know, Katie."

I opened the acquisition file, and instantly, something caught my attention. This was not the same document that was signed in Vegas. The terms had been changed, and a new clause was added. Immediately, I called Katie.

"Please get me the original paperwork for the acquisition of the hotel."

"You have it. It's on your desk."

"No, this isn't the original file," I spoke with concern.

"That's the only file there is, Gabby. I swear to you, that's the original."

Something wasn't right. It had all of our signatures on it, but it was not the same acquisition we signed. Son of a bitch. Someone was out to screw Young International. I closed the file and took the elevator up to Simon's office. I was literally shaking at the thought of seeing him, but I had no choice. The elevator doors opened, but his secretary wasn't at her desk. I didn't hesitate to push the door open and step in unannounced. The instant he heard the door open, he looked up at me from behind his desk. I gulped at the sight of him, but I couldn't let that deter me from why I was there. I was angry at him for personal reasons. This was business, and I had to keep it that way. I walked over to his desk and threw the file on it.

"Someone is trying to screw you over. Just thought you'd want to know." I turned around and headed for the door. Before I could reach it, he jumped up from his chair and slammed it shut, grabbed my face, and pushed me against the door as his mouth smashed into mine. He broke the kiss, and his piercing eyes stared into mine. I missed him. My strength was shattered by his kiss. I took in a deep breath as I tried to regain it.

"You're an asshole."

"I know, and I'm sorry."

My knees went weak as his eyes consumed me. He had that look. The look that I'd grown accustomed to. The look that wanted to devour my body. A sudden burst of sense flooded my mind as I pushed him away.

"Read the file. It's not the same document we signed."

I turned and walked out of his office, making a turn opposite the elevator and into the stairwell. After the door shut, I stood up against it, running my finger across my burning lips. I shook my head and headed back to my office.

∽

Jared and Giana were in the kitchen when I walked into my apartment.

"Gabs, is that you?" G yelled.

"Yes. Were you expecting someone else?"

"Get your ass in here. I can tell something's wrong,"

I took off my shoes and put my purse on the hallway table. As I stepped into the kitchen, Jared handed me a glass of wine and kissed me on the cheek.

"I think you need this."

"Thanks, Jared."

The smell of stir fry and rice overpowered the kitchen. I was starving. I had skipped lunch because my stomach was in knots over Simon.

"What happened today?"

I was vague because I didn't want to go into all the details. "It was just a bad day. Someone is trying to screw over Simon with the new hotel plans."

"Oh, that sucks. Does he know?"

"Yeah, I told him."

"So you saw him finally?" G asked with a smile.

"Only for a minute. I threw the file on his desk and walked out."

She gave me that "I know you're fucking lying" look that only a best friend would know. She set the stir fry on the table, and as soon as we sat down, there was a knock at the door.

"Are you expecting someone?" I asked.

"No. Are you?"

"No."

"I'll see who it is." I got up from my seat and walked to the door. I bet it was Donovan making a surprise visit to G. As soon as I opened the door, my heart stopped. My stomach fell as if I was going downhill on a roller coaster, and my eyes widened.

"Hello, Gabrielle."

"What are you doing here, Simon?" I asked as I swallowed hard.

"I need to talk to you."

"Then you should have called instead of just showing up at my apartment."

"Gabby, who is—Oh, Mr. Young. Come in." Giana smiled as she gently pushed me out of the way. "I'm Giana, Gabby's best friend and roommate."

"It's nice to finally meet you, Giana. Gabrielle has told me so much about you."

I wanted to fucking die. I was going to kill her!

"You're just in time for dinner. Please join us. I made

stir fry."

Seriously, she was fucking dead.

"Thank you. Don't mind if I do." Simon smiled as he looked at me.

I walked away and sat back down at the table. Giana introduced him to Jared and took the empty seat beside mine. A thousand reasons were going through my head as to why I should get up and leave, but I couldn't. I had to act as normal as possible for my own sake.

"So what brings you to our humble little home, Mr. Young?" G slyly asked.

"Please, call me Simon." He flashed his sexy smile at her. "I just needed to talk to Gabrielle about some business."

"You could have called," I sneered.

"You wouldn't have answered."

"You're right. I wouldn't have."

"Okay, well, I'm happy you're joining us for dinner." G smiled.

Jared, G, and Simon carried on conversations while I sat there, picking at my food. G had expressed her condolences to him, and he graciously thanked her. Wow. I didn't even get a thank you. All I got was an "I want to be alone. Don't bother me" response. The more I thought about it, the angrier I became.

"If you'll excuse me," I said as I got up, took my plate to the sink, and went to my bedroom, closing the door behind me.

It was only a matter of minutes before there was a knock on the door.

"Gabrielle, can I come in?"

I sighed. If I told him no, he would come in anyway. "Whatever, Simon."

He opened the door and shut it behind him as I sat on

my bed. "Stay right where you are," I commanded. "Say what you came here to say, and then you can leave."

He leaned up against the door with his hands in his pockets. I had to look away because the Simon ache had emerged, and the longer I looked at him and that sexy body of his, the more I would become vulnerable.

"I want to thank you for bringing that change in the acquisition to my attention. I'm having it investigated. Nobody would have seen that because only two words in the whole contract were changed. I could have lost millions."

"Well, lucky for you, I happen to have a photographic memory."

"Lucky for me, I have you," he spoke. "May I approach you?"

I couldn't believe the nerve of him. Acting like everything between us was okay. I got up from the bed and put up my hands.

"No! You may not approach me. Your behavior is completely unacceptable, even on a friend level. I reached out to you in your time of need, and you fucking turned your back on me."

"Gabrielle, I'm—"

"Sorry? I don't want your apology. I don't want anything from you. From this day forth, we have a complete business relationship, and that's it."

There was a knock at the door, and G poked her head in. "Umm...Jared and I are going to go out for a few drinks so the two of you can talk. I'll text you when I'm on my way home."

I nodded my head, and she shut the door.

"Gabrielle, can you please calm the fuck down and hear me out. There's more going on here than you know about."

I stormed past him, opened the door, and walked into the living room. "Don't you dare, Simon."

"You can yell at me all you like, but I won't yell back. I'm going to sit here on your couch until you calm down. You can call me names, scream in my face, and do whatever you want, but I will not fight back. That's not my style. Once you've gotten your anger for me out of your system, then we can talk."

"There's nothing to talk about. I don't want to hear anything you have to say. You just can't come back after ignoring me for a week and think that I'm okay. I sent you a text message on the day of your grandfather's funeral, and you ignored me."

"It was a rough day."

"Of course it was, and I wanted to be there for you. To comfort you as any friend would."

"What part of 'I wanted to be alone' did you not understand? I didn't want to be comforted."

I was finally beginning to calm down since I was the only one doing all the yelling. It wasn't getting me anywhere, so I just needed to stop.

"Okay. I understand that," I said in a calm voice. "But all you had to do was tell me that you were okay. That was all I wanted. I've been ignored my whole life, Simon. I spent six years being ignored by a man who supposedly loved me. I don't want to be ignored anymore. We're friends, and friends don't ignore each other." I was losing my strength, and I could feel myself slipping.

He held out his hand to me. "Come here, Gabrielle."

I took in a deep breath, and against my better judgment, I walked over and placed my hand in his. He pulled me down onto his lap and wrapped his arms around me, pulling me into him and softly stroking my hair.

"I'm sorry. I didn't mean to ignore you. Things are happening, and I can't stop them."

I sat up and looked at him. "What things?"

"You. I'm losing control, Gabrielle. You make me lose control. My grandfather's death scared me, not because he was gone, but because of how badly I needed you. I've never needed anyone before, and I don't know how to handle it. The other women in my life never mattered anything to me except sex. They gave me a physical pleasure, and that was it. You give me both physical and emotional pleasure."

I placed my hand on his cheek and gently brushed my lips against his. The words he spoke to me were words that had never been said to me before. He took away all the anger I had for him. I could feel his erection pressing against me while we kissed softly and lightly. I nipped at his bottom lip, and he moaned. He lifted me from his lap and carried me to my bedroom, laying me down on the bed and slowly unbuttoning my shirt. Once he unbuttoned the last one, he pushed my shirt open and slid his tongue along the center of my breasts. He wanted me as much as I wanted him and, at that moment, everything that had happened all week suddenly didn't matter anymore. His hand unbuttoned my pants and slid down the front of them, feeling my already-soaked panties.

"I love how wet you get," he whispered as his tongue slid across my ear. He got up and unbuttoned his shirt, sliding it off his shoulders and letting it drop to the ground. As he unbuttoned his pants and took them off, I stood up in front of him and did the same. His fingers reached behind me and unclasped my bra. With a hitched breath, he removed my bra and cupped my breasts in his hands.

"I could barely stand not being able to touch these

beautiful breasts and sticking my cock inside you all week. It's all I thought about."

"It's all I thought about too," I said with bated breath as he suckled my hard nipple. I arched my back as he placed the palm of his hand against my aching spot. He pressed firmly, moving his hand back and forth before dipping his fingers inside me. I gasped, and he carefully laid me down on the bed, manipulating my insides generously as he always did. His lips hovered steadily over mine as his eyes carefully watched the pleasurable expression on my face when his thumb hit my clit.

"You like that, don't you? I love to watch the faces you make while my fingers are inside of you, and I'm rubbing your swollen clit until you come undone. I love to watch your body unravel and surrender itself to me."

The words he spoke were all it took to send me over the edge and to the exhilarating orgasm that my body was ready for. Once my orgasm was finished, he immediately went down on me, spreading my legs further apart and securing his mouth around me. My legs tightened around his head as his tongue moved in and out of me. Coming up for air, he hovered over me, and without warning, he thrust deep inside of me.

"God, Gabrielle, you feel amazing." His lips were dangerously close to mine as my fingers tangled in his hair. "My cock craves you. I never thought it was possible to want to be inside of someone so much and so badly."

I brought his mouth down to mine and parted my lips, begging for his tongue. The long, feral kiss, the slick movements of his manhood thrusting in and out of me, our heavy breathing, and our racing hearts led us to climax together. He cried out my name as he pushed deep inside me, holding still while he released himself. Before collapsing on top of me, his lips touched mine.

Chapter Twenty-Three

"There's something I need to tell you," Simon said as he buttoned the last button on his shirt.

I didn't like his tone. It worried me. We had just had amazing sex, and now he had something to tell me.

"What is it?"

"Get dressed and pack your work clothes for tomorrow. I want you to spend the night at my house."

"No, Simon. Tell me first," I said as I grabbed his arm.

"Please, Gabrielle. Do this one thing for me."

"Fine. But you're scaring me."

"There's no need to be scared, baby." He took my face in his hands and kissed my head.

I threw on some clothes and packed a light bag. Giana texted me that she was down the hall and would be home in ten seconds. So much for her notice. As we walked out of the bedroom, Giana stepped into the apartment.

"Where are you going?" she asked as she looked down at my bag.

"She's spending the night at my house. I hope you don't mind."

"Who me? Mind? Are you kidding? Have fun! It was great to meet you, Simon." She smiled.

"It was my pleasure, Giana. Have a nice night."

He walked out, and she grabbed my arm before I could step out the door.

"It smells like sex in here. I see the two of you made up."

"Sort of." I smiled.

~

As soon as we stepped into Simon's house, he walked over to the bar and poured himself a scotch and me a glass of wine.

"What's going on?" I asked nervously.

"There's something you should know, and I want you to hear it from me before you hear it elsewhere. But first, I want us to clear a few things up. I like you, Gabrielle. I like you a lot, and I like spending time with you. I want us to spend more time together."

I thought I knew what he was saying without directly saying it, but I was still scared of what he had to tell me.

"Okay," I replied.

He threw back his scotch and brushed his hands through his hair. "Remember the woman you saw me with at the gala?"

"Yes," I answered.

"Her name is Alyssa Troth. She's pregnant, and she's claiming the baby is mine."

Swallowing hard, I took a seat on the chaise lounge that was closest to me and stared at him. My heart felt like it was going to jump out of my chest.

"I can promise you the baby isn't mine," Simon said as he stood in front of me.

"How do you know that? Why would she say that?"

"Because she wants to hook her claws into me for life."

"How can you be so sure you're not the father? You don't use condoms."

"I am sure. She's doing this on purpose. She's nuts."

"Stop." I put up my hands. "I can't listen to that. Jesus Christ, Simon," I spewed as I got up from the chaise.

I heard him sigh. "Gabrielle, please. I am not the father of her baby. The timing is all off. I'm going to prove it. But, in the meantime, people are going to talk. She'll go to the press and make me out to be some kind of monster if I don't cooperate. Listen, baby. I need your support in this. I need you to believe me and give me time to prove that she's lying."

"What exactly do you want from me? Spell it out, Simon!" I yelled.

"I want us to be together. You and me. That day in Vegas, after the meeting. The phone call I took wasn't only about my grandfather. It was about her as well. I couldn't tell you because I knew it would hurt you, and I shouldn't have cared if it hurt you, but I did. I cared too much, and I wanted to protect you. I tried to let you go, but I couldn't. Then, after my grandfather passed away, and I found myself needing you more and more, I thought if I distanced myself for a couple of days, the feelings would pass, but they didn't. The longer I was away from you, the deeper the feelings became. Fuck, Gabrielle! You've consumed me. You've taken over my fucking life."

I slowly closed my eyes as I stood there and listened to him. No strings. No emotions. He broke his own rules for me, and I was about to break mine. I walked over to where he stood and took hold of his hands.

"You and me, eh? Just the two of us? Until we can figure out a way to prove you're not the baby daddy."

He let out a small laugh. "Please don't call me the baby daddy. Are you in? It's going to be tough for a while."

"I'm in." I smiled as I brought my hand to his hair. "I'm tough. I can handle it. But I have one question for you. What happens if you are the father of her baby?"

"I'm not, Gabby," he whispered as he ran his thumb down my chin.

"You called me Gabby."

"I slipped." He smiled.

I reached up and brushed my lips against his. "Take me to the bedroom and show me how much you want me."

"Of course. But I don't think we'll make it to the bedroom. I'm thinking we may make it up the stairs, and that's about it."

"You're in control, Mr. Young. Take me wherever and however you want."

"Ah, you shouldn't have said that, Miss McCarthy." He winked.

∼

A month passed, and Simon and I spent a lot of time together. We would alternate between his house and my apartment. He had gotten to know G and Donovan better, and the four of us would have dinner and drinks together frequently. The baby drama was still happening, and Simon's people were no closer to finding the truth than they were two weeks ago. As for the mishap with the acquisition of the hotel, a man named Marcus, who was in cahoots with the previous hotel owner, was the one responsible for having the documents changed and making it look authentic so Simon would lose millions. It had something to do with Simon's grandfather and some bad business deal with the family twenty years ago.

Simon and I were sitting on the couch, watching a movie, when G and Donovan stormed in.

"Giana, I promise I'm going to tell her as soon as she gets back from Montreal."

"You've been saying that for how many months now? You're a liar. I don't believe you intend ever to leave her," G yelled.

They both went to the bedroom and shut the door. Things had been kind of tense the past week for them. Giana had confided in me that maybe she was wrong about Donovan and that he was never leaving his wife. I sat up with her a few nights ago while she cried on my shoulder over him.

"Well, that was awkward," Simon spoke.

"Yeah. Just a bit. Do you think he's ever going to leave his wife?"

"I do. A man in his position needs to make sure everything is secure, and I'm sure that's what he's waiting for. Plus, with him being a lawyer, I wouldn't put it past him to hide some accounts and move money around."

"I hope for G's sake, he does it quick." I laid my head down on Simon's lap and looked up at him. "Your people need to hurry up and find some dirt on Alyssa."

"They will, baby. This stuff takes time." He smiled as he ran his finger along my cheek. "Thank you."

"For what?"

"For believing me and sticking by me. You're pretty special. Did you know that?"

"I think so." I grinned.

"Is that so?" Simon began to tickle me as I felt his erection against the back of my head.

"Is your cock ever not hard?"

The Secret He Holds

"Is your pussy ever not wet?"

"*Touché*, Mr. Young. Can I spend the night at your house tonight?"

"Why?" he asked. "I mean, of course, you can, but we never spend the night together unless it's the weekend."

"I think maybe I should let G and Donovan have the apartment to themselves tonight. With his wife being out of town, I'm sure he's staying the night, and by the sound of things, they'll be up all night talking."

"That's a good idea. Go grab your things, and we'll drive your car back so I don't have to call Patrick."

We had just finished making love when Simon's phone rang. As he reached over and took it from the nightstand, he looked at me and rolled his eyes.

"Hello, Alyssa. It's rather late, don't you think? I'm sorry, but I can't tomorrow. I'm tied up in meetings all day with the new hotel. No. It's not up for discussion, Alyssa. Go to bed. We'll talk tomorrow."

"What was all that about?" I asked as I snuggled up against him.

"She's going for an ultrasound tomorrow and expected me to be there. Don't give it another thought, Gabrielle," he said as he kissed my head. "Let's get some sleep."

As I lay there wrapped in his arms, I couldn't help but wonder if Alyssa was telling the truth and Simon was the father of her baby. If he was, could I deal with it? I didn't know. I didn't know what the future held, and I didn't want to think about it. I only wanted to live in the present moment, where I was the happiest I'd ever been in my entire life.

Chapter Twenty-Four

"Katie, can you call up to Mr. Young's office and see if he's in? I need to go over some plans with him."

"Yes, he's up there," she replied.

I grabbed the folder and plans from my desk and took the elevator up to Simon's office.

"Knock, knock." I smiled as I lightly opened the door. "Do you have a few minutes?"

"For you, I have eternity." He smiled.

I entered his office and took a seat across from his desk. As we sat there and discussed the renovations, his door opened. The look of disdain on his face forced me to turn around, only to see Alyssa walking in.

"What is she doing here?" she asked with hatred in her voice.

"She's my employee, and we're in a meeting. You don't just walk into my office unannounced."

"Your secretary wasn't at her desk. I came to show you something since you never bothered to show up for the ultrasound."

"I told you that I was in meetings all day."

She pulled a small piece of paper out of her purse. "It's a boy. You're going to have a son, darling." She smiled as she walked over and kissed his cheek.

"I'll give you two happy parents a moment," I spoke as I began to get up from my seat.

"No. Stay. We have to finish this meeting. Alyssa, we'll talk later."

"Do you know what this means, Simon? You're going to have a son to carry on the Young legacy. Aren't you the least bit excited?"

"Congratulations." I smiled.

"Thank you. We are so happy. Aren't we, baby?" she said as she placed her hands firmly on his shoulders.

I thought Simon was going to lose it as anger consumed his eyes.

"If you'll excuse me for a moment, I forgot something in my office." I needed to get out of there. I went to the bathroom and into the stall. A few moments later, I heard the bathroom door open and the clicking of heels on the tile floor. Suddenly, I heard Alyssa's voice.

"Hello, this is Hilary Stout. You left a message earlier letting me know that Dr. Jennings had a cancellation this afternoon. Yes, I have the ultrasound report with me. Thank you. I'll see you at four o'clock."

She stepped into the stall next to me, and I quickly flushed the toilet and left the bathroom before she could see me. Why the hell did she give a different name? What was she up to? I ran down the four flights of stairs back to my office and did a Google search for Dr. Jennings. He was an OB/GYN.

"Ahem," I heard from the doorway. "You never came back to my office. What's going on?" he asked as he stepped inside.

I got up from my desk and grabbed his arm, pulling him inside my office and shutting the door.

"Get in here."

"Baby, remember, we're keeping it on the down low at the office."

"Stop it. Listen to me. After I left your office, I went to the bathroom. As I was in the stall, Alyssa walked in and made a phone call. She called a Dr. Jennings and said her name was Hilary Stout."

"What? Why the hell would she give a fake name?"

"Obvious reasons, Simon. She didn't want to be found out. Which means the baby isn't yours." I smiled.

"I told you all along it wasn't. That stupid bitch." He cupped his hands around my ass and pulled me closer to him. "Now I can end this once and for all." He smiled as he kissed my lips. "I have some phone calls to make. I'll see you later."

He gave me one last kiss and walked out of my office.

~

I stepped into the apartment. G and Donovan were sitting on the couch in a warm embrace, which I thought was odd since they were home earlier than usual.

"Hey." I walked through the door and set my phone and keys on the hallway table.

"Oh, hi," G replied with a smile. "We're ordering Chinese. Are you sticking around for dinner?"

"Sure. Let me text Simon and see if he wants to come over."

I grabbed my phone from the table and sent him a text message.

The Secret He Holds

"We're ordering Chinese for dinner. Are you game?"

"Go ahead and eat without me. I'm meeting with some people in a while about Alyssa. I'll call you later."

"Okay."

"I'm fantasizing about that sweet ass of yours and what I want to do to it. I'm hard already."

"Lol. You'll have to wait until later. Maybe you should have taken me in your private bathroom earlier, and I could have given you my ass and your fantasy."

"Stop. Now I'm going to have to jack off before my meeting. Send me a pic of your tits."

"No! Use your imagination."

"You're cruel, Gabrielle."

"Bye, Simon."

I smiled as I set down my phone. "He has a meeting, so he won't be here. I'll go grab the menu from the kitchen."

After placing the order, the restaurant said they were so busy that it would be over an hour and a half before they could deliver the food, so I told G and Donovan that I would pick it up.

"I can go," Donovan said.

"Nah, it's okay. You two stay here, and I'll get it. I don't mind."

I walked to the bedroom and changed out of my work clothes and into more comfortable clothing. I grabbed my keys, and as I was headed out the door, Donovan stopped me.

"Here, I'm buying." He smiled as he handed me some money.

"No. I got it. Don't worry about it. Let me treat you and G this time."

"Take it. We're celebrating tonight."

"Oh really? What are we celebrating?"

"I told my wife that I was filing for a divorce last night."

"Oh. How did she take it?"

"Better than I thought she would. I was really surprised."

"That's great, Donovan. I'm happy for you. But dinner's on me tonight." I pushed his hand away and walked out the door.

The Chinese restaurant was about twenty minutes away. There was one right around the corner from the apartment, but it wasn't as good. I was really happy that Donovan finally got the balls to leave his wife. Now, maybe he and G could start building a future together. It often made me wonder if he would do the same to her one day. Since the day I met her, she had never shown this much interest in one guy. I finally arrived at the restaurant, picked up the carry-out, and headed back to the apartment.

"I'm back," I said as I opened the door, and my keys dropped to the floor. When I bent down to pick them up, I noticed a trail of liquid on the dark wood floor. "What the hell?" I said as I touched it with my finger and saw that it was pure red. My heart began racing, and I started to shake. "G. Donovan?" I screamed as I threw down the bag. The trail led me to the kitchen, where Donovan was lying on the floor. With shaking hands, I ran over to him and put my ear to his mouth. He was barely breathing and lying unconscious. "Giana," I screamed as tears flowed down my face. I got up and ran through the apartment, and that was when I saw Giana lying face down in a pool of blood in the hallway. Screams rang through the apartment as I rolled her over.

"Giana, Giana," I screamed.

I ran to the door where I had left my purse, grabbed my cell phone, and dialed 911.

"My best friend and her boyfriend have been shot. Please send someone here quickly. Hurry!"

I rattled off the address and ran back to G. Her eyes were barely open as I applied as much pressure as I could to her gunshot wound. With my other hand, I dialed Simon.

"I'm in a meeting. I'll call you when I'm done," he answered.

"NO!" I screamed. "Oh my God!"

"Gabby, what's wrong?"

I could barely say the words. My voice was shaking, and I was hysterical. "G and Donovan were shot in the apartment. Simon, oh my God, help me!" I sobbed.

"I'm on my way." Click.

G reached up and grabbed my arm.

"Who did this, G?"

"Sylvia," she whispered.

I heard the door open, and I got up and ran to the paramedics and police who had entered.

"Donovan is in the kitchen, and Giana is in the hall," I cried.

I was covered in blood. My hands were dripping as I stood there in shock. A police officer named Brent covered me with a blanket.

"Do you know who did this?" he asked.

I was shaking uncontrollably, and my lip was quivering. "Giana told me it was Sylvia, Donovan's wife."

"Do you know their last name?" he asked.

"Holmes. Sylvia Holmes."

Brent walked away and got on his radio. I could hear the chaos throughout the apartment.

"Gabrielle," Simon shouted as he entered the apartment. I looked at him with a blank stare as he bent down and grabbed my bloodstained hands. "Baby, oh my God." He pulled me into an embrace and held my head against his chest. "Jesus Christ, who did this?"

"Sylvia," I said in a daze.

"Donovan's wife?"

"That's what G said."

Before I knew it, Brent, the officer, was standing in front of me. "Miss, I'm sorry, but I have to ask you a few more questions."

I lifted my head and nodded.

"Officer, you can clearly see she's in shock. Can it wait?"

"No. I'm sorry, but it's still fresh in her mind. We need as much information right now. Can you tell me where you were during the attack?"

With a quivering lip, I answered him. "I was out picking up our dinner from the Chinese restaurant. I was only gone for forty minutes and found them when I returned."

"Okay. Well, we have to seal this apartment off as a crime scene. Do you have somewhere else you can stay?"

"She'll stay with me. I'm her boyfriend."

"Okay. Then I'll need your phone number and address so we can get in contact with her if we have additional questions."

I looked over as I heard the wheels of the stretchers across the floor. I jumped up and ran over to G.

"Is she alive?" I cried.

"Yes, ma'am, but she's very critical. We need to get her to the hospital quickly."

"And him?"

"He's barely holding on. I'm sorry."

The Secret He Holds

Simon grabbed me as I fell to the ground. "Can she at least get cleaned up?" he asked the officer.

"Not here. I'm sorry, but we can't have anything disturbed."

Simon grabbed my purse and my phone and carried me out of the apartment.

"I have to go to the hospital. I can't leave her."

"Shh...baby. I'm taking you back to my place first to get cleaned up, and then I'll take you over to the hospital."

The hallways of the building were cluttered with people trying to see what had happened. Bright flashing police lights blinded me as Simon carried me to his car. All the way to his house, I didn't say a word. My head leaned against the window as I stared into the night. I was numb. When we arrived at his house, he carried me from the car and upstairs to his bathroom. He made me sit on the toilet while he started a bath.

"I don't want to take a bath," I whispered.

"You need to get yourself cleaned up if you want to go to the hospital."

He lifted me from the toilet, undressed me, and then helped me into the bath. Grabbing the loofah sponge from the corner, he poured some of the lavender-scented shower gel that I kept there on it and slowly caressed my skin, focusing mainly on my hands.

"Everything's going to be okay. They are going to pull through and make it."

"You don't know that. What if she dies?" I began to sob.

"She's not going to die, Gabrielle."

"I have to be with her. I have to go to the hospital, Simon." I started to get extremely upset.

"Calm down. I'm almost finished cleaning you up, and then we'll go."

Simon helped me out of the tub and wrapped an oversized towel around my body. He walked over to the drawer that I had taken over as I left some clothes behind from my weekly sleepovers. As I dressed, he changed into different clothes. I sat on the edge of the bed in a daze until he helped me up, and we went to the hospital.

Chapter Twenty-Five

When we arrived at the hospital, both Giana and Donovan were in surgery. We took a seat in the surgical waiting room, and Simon fetched us some coffee.

"Here, darling." He handed me a cup.

"Thanks."

He took the seat next to me and took hold of my hand. I was exhausted as I laid my head on his shoulder. When I awoke, I was lying down on the couch with a blanket over me, and Simon was standing by the window on the phone. I sat up and had to focus on where I was at. I had prayed it was nothing but a nightmare, but it wasn't. Simon turned around and looked at me as he hung up from his phone call.

"Any news yet?"

"No, I just checked with the nurse, and they both just got out of surgery."

"What time is it?"

"Six a.m.," he replied as he kissed my head.

"Gabrielle McCarthy?" a man in surgical scrubs asked as he walked into the waiting room.

"Yes." I stood up.

"The bullet that hit Giana was lodged in her chest cavity. We were able to remove it with minimal complications, but she lost a lot of blood. We have her on a ventilator, and the next forty-eight hours are critical, but she should make a full recovery."

"And Donovan?" I asked.

"You'll have to talk to his doctor. I'll go find him. Meanwhile, if you would like to see your friend, you may."

We followed the doctor down the hallway and into Giana's room. I gasped and covered my mouth when I looked at her from the doorway. She was pale. The tubes coming from her were hooked up to machines that produced a steady stream of beeps. Simon clasped my shoulders and guided me over to her bedside. Tears fell down my face as I took hold of her hand.

"I'm here, G. You're going to be okay."

Another doctor walked through the door to update us on Donovan. "We were able to remove the bullet from his chest and control the bleeding. Due to the severe swelling of his brain from the trauma he sustained when he fell, we had to put him in a medically induced coma and wait for the swelling to subside."

"Is there any brain damage?" Simon asked.

"We won't know until he wakes up, which could be days or even weeks. Your friend was lucky that whoever fired that shot missed his heart."

"Thank you, doctor," I said as I turned and looked at Giana.

"They're both alive, Gabrielle. That's the most important thing," Simon said as he wrapped his arms around me.

The Secret He Holds

A nurse walked in and smiled as she checked Giana's vitals. "You two look exhausted. Why don't you go home and get some sleep? I'll call you if there are any changes."

"What if she wakes up? She'll be alone and scared," I said.

"Sweetheart, she isn't going to be waking up for a long time. Don't worry. She's in good hands here. You can come back later tonight. Come on, baby. You need to eat something as well as get some sleep. You heard the nurse. She'll be in good hands."

After stopping in and checking on Donovan, Simon drove us back to his house.

"Go upstairs and climb into bed. I'll have Martha make us something to eat."

"I'm not hungry."

He placed his hand on my chin. "It doesn't matter if you're hungry or not; you need to eat. Now go."

I sighed and walked up the stairs. I pulled back his comforter and climbed underneath, gripping the edge tightly and pulling it up to my chin. She was going to be okay. I had to believe that. I couldn't lose her. Not now, not ever. Simon walked into the room and handed me a cup of tea.

"I thought you could use some."

"Thank you," I softly spoke, taking the cup from his hands.

Just as Simon sat on the bed next to me, Martha knocked on the door.

"Mr. Young, there is a policeman here to speak to Miss McCarthy."

He sighed. "Thank you, Martha. Tell him she'll be right down. Are you okay to go down and answer his questions?"

"Yeah. I'll be fine."

I climbed out of bed and brought my tea down with me. Brent, the officer from last night, was sitting in a chair in the living room.

"Officer," Simon said.

"Hello. I wanted to stop by and let you know that we apprehended Mrs. Holmes, and she confessed to everything. We won't be needing you for further questioning."

"That's great. Thank you for stopping by and letting me know."

"My pleasure, ma'am, and I'm sorry about your friends. How are they?"

"Critical at the moment. Only time will tell."

"You both have a good day."

"Thank you, officer," Simon said as he escorted him out.

Simon put his arm around me, and we went back upstairs. "I have something to tell you."

My already fucked up stomach sank. "Now what?" I sighed.

"Relax, darling. I'm not the father of Alyssa's baby. Just like I told you I wasn't."

"For absolute sure?"

"Yes." He smiled.

I climbed back into bed and snuggled against Simon.

"She went and saw a specialist, some IVF doctor, and had sperm implanted in her by a donor."

"WHAT?!" I exclaimed as I lifted my head.

"I know. She's really fucked up. She did it under a different name for which she went to great lengths to create this fake identity."

"Didn't she stop to think that you'd find out?"

"She's crazy, Gabrielle. I don't know what she thought."

"Have you talked to her about it?"

"No. I sent my people to confront her and tell her that if she didn't leave town immediately, I would go to the authorities to report her for assuming a fake identity. Not only could she wind up in jail, but she'd more than likely lose her baby. Not that it would be such a bad thing because who would want that looney tunes for a mother?"

"You didn't give her money, did you?"

"No, baby. I didn't give her anything. Just a swift kick in the ass out of town. She will never contact me again." He smiled as his lips brushed against mine. "Now close your eyes and get some rest."

"Will you stay with me?" I asked desperately.

"Of course, I'll stay with you. I'm tired myself."

I laid my head down on his rock-solid chest and closed my eyes. At least one thing was settled. Now, we could act like a couple in public—no more hiding.

"One more thing before we go to sleep," I softly spoke.

"What is it?"

"Last night, you told the officer that you were my boyfriend. Is that what we are?"

His grip around me tightened. "I believe we are, and I'm happy to say that you're my first girlfriend, Gabrielle."

A wide smile splayed across my face. I wanted to tell him I loved him, but I couldn't. I was too scared to say it first. He said I was his girlfriend and that we were a couple, but those three words were never spoken by either of us.

Chapter Twenty-Six

I'd spent every night after work at the hospital for the past week. G had woken up three days after the shooting and was having a hard time with everything. Her hospital room was filled with flowers from the law firm and many cards wishing her a speedy recovery. Donovan was still in a coma, and G cried every day. Simon and I tried to keep her as calm as we could. He pulled some strings and got the two of them in the same room together. That way, G could talk to Donovan whenever she wanted. Even though he was in a coma, the nurse said he could still hear things. I was still staying at Simon's house because I couldn't bear to return to the apartment. Simon had hired a cleaning crew to go over and clean up the mess so that when G was released from the hospital, everything would be in order. He was an amazing boyfriend and a very generous man. He went with me every night to visit Giana and Donovan, and then we'd go back to his house and make love. Things couldn't have been more perfect with us. He still liked his control, and he didn't hesitate to let me know it, but that was okay because I was falling more in love with him every day.

Another month had passed, and Giana and Donovan were getting stronger. The three of us had moved into a different apartment because G refused to go back to the one we had, and the two of them couldn't bear to be apart. I had told her I would get my own place, but they insisted that I move in with them, at least temporarily, until they were both a hundred percent better. It was not like I was there all that much anyway. I spent more nights at Simon's house that I practically lived there. Word had gotten out at Young International that Simon and I were seeing each other, and he smiled proudly as he walked through the building.

"Why are you sulking?" G asked as stepped into my bedroom.

"I miss Simon."

"He's only been gone a day. When is he due back?"

"Tomorrow night."

"What's he doing in New York anyway?"

"Business meeting."

"Since tomorrow is Friday, why don't you fly to New York and surprise him? That way, you two can spend the weekend there and do some shopping."

"I don't know. New York isn't my favorite place anymore," I replied, putting on my jacket.

"Oh please, Gabby. If you're afraid of running into Dickwad, don't be. The city is huge. Anyway, if you did run into him, you'd be on the arm of a sexy billionaire. Wouldn't you want to show that off?"

"True. Maybe I will." I turned and smiled at her. "I can fly out first thing tomorrow morning."

"Good girl. Have a good day at work, and I'll see you later."

On my way to work, I stopped at Starbucks and picked up coffee for me and Katie.

"Good morning." I smiled as I set the cup on her desk.

"Thanks, Gabby."

"Come into my office, please," I said as I walked in and set my purse down. "I need you to book me on the first flight out to New York tomorrow morning. I'm going to surprise Simon."

"Ah, he'll love that. Do you know where he's staying? I can find out for you."

"He's at his hotel in Manhattan."

"Great. I'll go book your flight now."

As she walked out, I turned on my computer, and a collage of pictures I had taken of the two of us welcomed me on the screen. A few moments later, I heard my ringing phone. It was Simon.

"Hi there," I answered.

"Good morning, baby. Did you sleep well last night?"

"As well as could be expected without your arms wrapped around me."

"Ah, I know. I missed you in my bed last night, too. But I'll be home tomorrow night, and I promise to make it up to you. We'll spend the entire weekend in bed."

"Sounds good. I can't wait."

"I'll talk to you later. I just wanted to hear your sexy voice. Have a good day, Gabrielle. Don't miss me too much."

"Impossible. Have a good day." *Click*.

Later that night, Simon and I texted back and forth. I had to devise a plan because I wouldn't be answering his calls or messages while I was on the five-hour flight to New York.

"I have to take G to the doctor tomorrow so she can get clearance to go back to work, and then we're going to breakfast. I'll text you when I get to the office mid-morning."

"Okay. Have fun and give her and Donovan my best. One more night, baby. One more night, and then I'm all yours."

~

I took the five a.m. flight out of Seattle. I made my way through the airport, grabbed my luggage, and then took a cab to Simon's hotel. Nerves had taken over as I rode through the city that held memories I didn't want to revisit. When the driver pulled up to the curb, the valet opened the cab door and fetched my bag from the back.

"Hello. Will you be staying with us?" he politely asked.

"Yes. I'm Gabrielle McCarthy from Young International."

"Welcome." He gave me a warm smile as he held open the door for me.

When I stepped inside the luxurious lobby, I walked up to the front desk.

"Hello, and good day. How may I help you?"

"I'm Gabrielle McCarthy from Young International, and I will be staying in Mr. Young's suite."

"Does Mr. Young know you've arrived?"

"No. I'm his girlfriend, and it's a surprise."

"I'm sorry, miss, but I can't grant you access to Mr. Young's suite without notifying him that you're here."

I cocked my head. "Really? Do you think I'm lying or something?"

"Please understand where I'm coming from. You aren't the only woman who has claimed to be Mr. Young's girlfriend to get into his suite."

Was he serious right now?

"Okay. I'll just wait for him elsewhere, and you can be sure that I will tell him how you wouldn't let me, his GIRLFRIEND, in his suite," I said with a shaking finger.

"I'm really sorry, but I'm only doing my job."

"Can you at least hold my luggage for me until he comes back?" I asked.

"Of course I can." He took my luggage, and I went and sat down in one of the oversized, comfy grey chairs in the lobby.

As I scrolled through my phone, checking emails and messages from the office, I heard a voice from a distance that I never wanted to hear again. I slowly looked up, and two sets of eyes locked with mine: Simon and Brendon. They both halted, not taking another step, as they both stared at me. My heart started to pound out of my chest, and I felt sick to my stomach. What the fuck was Simon doing with my ex-boyfriend? I got up from the chair and unsteadily walked over to them.

"Oh shit," Brendon mumbled.

"Gabrielle, what are you doing here?" Simon asked in shock, and suddenly, a look of fear swept over his face.

"Hey, Gabby," Brendon said as he put his hands in his pockets and looked down.

"Hey, Gabby?" I spoke in anger at Brendon. "Fuck you!"

Brendon looked over at Simon. "Sorry, man." He began to walk away. I reached over and grabbed his arm, jerking him back to me.

"What do you mean 'sorry'? What the fuck is going on here?"

He slowly shook his head. "I told you that you were a pawn in someone's hand before you left."

I stood there in shock. I let go of his arm, and he

walked away. I slowly turned to Simon as he took in a sharp breath.

"WELL?!" I yelled.

"Not here, Gabrielle. In my suite, now!" he commanded.

The man behind the desk looked at me with a sympathetic look. I was shaking, and my mind was racing. Simon took hold of my arm lightly, and I jerked away from him. The last thing I wanted was for him to touch me.

"Don't you dare fucking touch me."

We stepped inside the elevator, and Simon inserted his key to take us up to the top floor. When the doors opened, he unlocked the door that was directly across. He held open the door, and I walked in, still shaking uncontrollably. I flinched when I heard the door shut.

"First of all, you need to calm down," he said.

"Calm down? You expect me to be calm when I just saw you with the person I hate the most on the face of the earth? You have seconds, and I mean seconds, to explain yourself."

He walked over to the bar that sat in the corner of the suite and poured himself a drink.

"Do you want one?" he asked.

"No, I don't want one!"

He threw back his scotch and took in a deep breath. "I was going to tell you. I swear I was. But it never seemed like the right time."

Chapter Twenty-Seven

SIMON

The way he talked to her was vile, and it took everything I had not to get out of my seat and punch him in the face. The things he said. His refusal to help her. The sad look that was embedded in her beautiful brown eyes. Eyes that met mine and instantly captivated me. She was a beautiful woman, and I wished she was alone. I couldn't stop staring at her and stealing small glances as she sat across the aisle seat. I scanned her finger, and she wasn't wearing a ring so that asshole must have been her boyfriend.

When the plane landed, I let her get out of her seat first, then walked behind her, checking out her fine ass and body that the asshole she was with put down. As soon as I climbed into the limo and shut the door, I watched her stare at me as the driver pulled away. I made a few phone calls and found out who both of them were. I spent days and even weeks thinking about Gabrielle McCarthy. She didn't deserve to be treated the way she was, and she didn't deserve to be stuck in a toxic relationship. I desired her. All of her. Gabrielle McCarthy was a woman who needed to be saved, and I was the one who was going to save her.

"Mr. Young, to what do I owe the pleasure of being summoned to this meeting?" Brendon asked as he sat down across from me.

"I took the liberty of ordering you a scotch. You seem to me like the scotch type of guy."

"I do like scotch. It's not my favorite, but it'll do," he smirked as he held the glass in his hand.

I glared at him from across the table, not sure of what he would think about my proposal. "So, you work for your father, and he's grooming you to take over the family business. Am I right?"

"You are correct, sir."

I sighed at his smugness. "I would like to make a business proposition. Imagine your father's reaction if I were to hire your company to oversee the development of one of my new hotels."

"Excuse me?" He nearly choked as he sat up straight.

"You heard me. You would look like a hero securing one of Young International's hotels."

He sat back in his chair and rested his arm on the table. "I have to question your motives, Mr. Young. I get the impression you're not doing this out of the kindness of your heart. What exactly do you want from *me*?"

"Your girlfriend, Gabrielle," I spoke as I arched my brow.

"Are you fucking serious?" He chuckled. "You're offering me a huge deal to develop one of your multi-billion-dollar hotels in exchange for Gabby?"

"Yes," I said calmly.

"Why? She's worth nothing."

It took everything I had not to jump across the table and beat the shit out of him.

"She is to me. Let me be candid with you, Brendon. You're an asshole, and Gabrielle doesn't deserve to be in the company of someone like you."

"Really? But she deserves to be with *you*? I know your background, Simon, and you'd do more harm to her than I ever could."

"You're wrong about that. Do we have a deal or not?"

"You're serious? This really isn't a joke."

"A joke, it's not. I don't kid around." I started to get up from my seat. "Let me know when you've decided. You have twenty-four hours. After that, the deal is gone."

"Wait!" he said. "Sit down, and let's discuss exactly how you want this handled."

I wasn't surprised that he would give her up so easily. He was that type of guy.

I sat down and signaled the waitress for another scotch. "I will have my attorney draw up the agreement between your company and my hotel tonight. You have one week to break it off with her. If you don't, then your company will lose my hotel. I don't care how you do it; just make sure she leaves you. It's beyond me how she's stayed with you this long anyway."

"Hey," he said.

"Once you break it off, you are never to contact her again. Are we clear?"

"Yeah, we're clear. How are you going to get her for yourself? Are you just going to sweep in after she leaves and take her home with you? Because I can guarantee she won't stay in New York. There is one place she'll run to."

"Where's that?" I asked as I interlaced my fingers.

"Seattle. Her best friend lives there. It's the only other friend she has. She's a royal bitch. But that's where Gabby will run."

The corners of my mouth curved upward as my plan

was now perfected. "I'll be in touch with you tomorrow," I said as I got up from my seat. "I can trust you will never mention this to anyone?"

"Are you kidding? Do you know how that would make me look? I have an image to uphold."

"Just remember, I can take it all away as fast as I gave it to you."

As I began to walk away, he called my name. As I turned around, he cocked his head and narrowed his eyes. "What kind of game are you playing?"

"The one where I'm the winner." I buttoned my suit coat and casually walked out of the restaurant.

∼

"Miss Howe, thank you for meeting me on such short notice." I smiled as I stood up and lightly shook her hand.

"My pleasure, Mr. Young. I must say, I was quite surprised to get your call."

"Please, call me Simon."

"Now tell me what Holster can do for Young International."

"I want you to fire one of your employees."

"What? You can't be serious?"

"I'm very serious, Kendra."

"Which employee?"

"Gabrielle McCarthy."

"She's one of our best employees."

"I know, and she'll be better at Young International."

"I'm sorry, Simon, but you have me confused. If you want to hire her, why don't you just call her up and offer her a job?"

"It's complicated, and it's not that simple. Let me ask

you something. What do you know about her boyfriend, Brendon Sommers?"

"Other than he's a complete asshole who deserves to be sent to the depths of Hell and never to be seen again, not much. Why?"

"Just curious."

She pursed her lips together as she narrowed her eyes at me. "You like her. Don't you?"

"It depends on what you mean by 'like.' Wouldn't you like to see her get out of her situation with Brendon? Start over and make a new life for herself?"

"Well, of course. I've been trying to get her to leave him for the past year, but she's too insecure. She keeps making excuses for this demeaning and degrading behavior."

"Then fire her or lay her off. Give her a chance at a new life."

"A life that involves you?" She smiled.

"Of course. She'd be working for me."

"Unfortunately, we just lost a big department store account, and we have to lay off five people. But Gabby wasn't one of them. We were actually going to promote her to a marketing manager because she's an amazing employee."

"Well, now it looks like you'll be laying her off. Listen, if you do this small favor for me, I will give you the marketing account for my hotel in the Virgin Islands to help with the loss of your department store account."

"You'd do that?"

"I'm a man of my word. I can have my attorney draw up the contract today."

"I suppose she would be better off in Seattle. Her best friend lives there, and they're really close. It would be good for her to start a new life there."

"Then it's settled." I stood up and lightly shook her hand. "I'll have my associate, Peter, give you a call to get Gabrielle's number, and I'll call you when I know she's in Seattle. I can trust you will never mention this to anyone."

"I would never. As far as I'm concerned, this meeting never took place."

"Thank you. I'll be in touch soon." As I began to walk past her, she placed her hand on my arm.

"She's a really good person. Please don't hurt her."

"I won't," I said with a small smile.

My plan was now set in motion, full circle, and soon she'd be in Seattle, where she belonged.

Chapter Twenty-Eight

GABRIELLE

"What the fuck is that supposed to mean?!" I yelled from across the room. "What were you going to tell me?"!

I was seriously clueless at this point. The only thing I could think of was that he was working with Brendon on a business deal, and he was scared to tell me.

He ran his fingers through his hair and inhaled deeply.

"TELL ME!" I screamed.

The next thing I knew, he threw his glass against the wall. "Fine. You want to know so badly, I'll tell you. I was the one responsible for you coming to Seattle!" he shouted.

I stood there in shock, trying to wrap my head around his words. "What?" I asked quietly as I shook my head.

He closed his eyes for a moment before answering me. His voice lowered. "I made a business deal with Brendon to make you leave him in exchange for his company overseeing the construction of one of my new hotels. I arranged it all." He turned away from me.

"What? Why?" I began to shake fiercely.

"For you. You didn't deserve to be treated like that. He

didn't deserve you. You looked so unhappy and so sad. It affected me, Gabrielle. In a big way. From the moment I laid eyes on you, I knew I needed to save you."

"Save me?" Tears started to pour down my face. "Who the fuck are you? God? Do you know why I left him? Do you know what he did?"

He shook his head. "No. I told him I didn't want to know."

I walked over to where he stood and grabbed his arm, forcing him to look at me. "Then let me enlighten you!" I said through gritted teeth. "I came home to him fucking another woman in our bed! Do you know what that did to me to see that? DO YOU?!"

"I'm so sorry." He reached for my hand, and I backed away.

I closed my eyes tightly for a moment and prepared myself for his answer to my next question.

"Did you have anything to do with me getting laid off from my job?"

He looked at me with tears in his eyes. "Yes."

I threw my hands over my mouth and sank to my knees. It felt like a thousand knives were being thrown at me.

"Gabrielle, are you okay?" He knelt down in front of me.

"Don't touch me."

"I need you to listen to me. Please. What I did was wrong, but you were never going to leave him. You told me you endured that emotional abuse for six years. Six years, Gabby, and day by day, he took everything away from you. I couldn't let you go through that anymore. He gave you up for a damn business deal. I brought you to Seattle and gave you everything you lost. I gave myself to you completely, which I'd never done before. I knew you were different from anyone I'd ever known, but I didn't expect to fucking fall in love with you. I saved you! You have to see that. I'm so sorry, baby. Please, I'm begging you. Please forgive me."

I broke out into a full-blown cry as I sat there on the ground. "Do you think because you have money that you can fuck with people's lives? Do you?" I cried as I pushed him.

He grabbed hold of my wrists as tears started to stream down his face. "I saved you. I love you, Gabrielle."

"You don't love me. You aren't capable of love. What you did is—God, there are no words for what you did, and then to keep it from me after everything we'd been through. If I hadn't come here and seen the two of you, you would never have told me. You would have kept your dirty, filthy little secret for the rest of your life, and I would have lived every day believing that you were someone different. Someone who would never use their money or power to buy people. God, I can't even believe this," I cried as I placed my hands over my eyes.

"I'm different. You changed everything in my life. Why can't you see that?"

"All I see is a calculated and manipulating man. We're over! Do you fucking understand those words?!" I stood up and grabbed my purse. As I placed my hand on the door handle, I turned and looked at him.

"You said you saved me from Brendon. Now I'm saving myself from you." As soon as I walked out the door, I heard him scream my name.

I stepped into the elevator and looked at myself in the mirror. My eyes were glossy and mascara-stained. I went to the desk, and the man who helped me earlier immediately handed me my bag from behind the counter.

"I'm so sorry, miss."

I wiped my eyes, took my bag, and climbed into a cab.
"Hey, are you okay, lady?" the driver asked.
"No. I'm not. JFK, please."

~

People were staring at me as I walked through the airport. My flight didn't leave for an hour, so I went inside the bathroom to clean up my face. As I pulled the pack of face-cleansing wipes from my carry-on bag, I placed it on my face and stared at myself in the mirror. I was broken, more broken than I'd ever been in my existence. I began to wipe the mascara from under my eyes. The betrayal I felt was nothing I'd ever felt before. The pain was unbearable, and the tears wouldn't stop flowing as I washed my face. I placed my hands on the counter and stood back with my head down, trying to find a way to make the pain stop with every breath I took.

"Are you all right?" a little old lady asked as she placed her hand on my back.

"I'm just not feeling well. I'll be fine."

"Do you need me to get someone for you, dear?"

"No. I just need a moment."

She walked away, and I sat on the bench against the wall in the airport bathroom. If Simon was coming for me, he couldn't come in here. I waited until I heard the boarding call for my flight. I sat down in the seat, and as soon as the plane took off, I placed the pillow against the window and closed my eyes.

~

I stepped into the apartment, ready to collapse, when G emerged from the kitchen.

"Gabby, what the hell?" She ran over to me.

I grabbed her arms for support and slowly fell to the ground. She followed and wrapped her arms around me.

"What happened?"

"It's over between Simon and me, and I never want to see him again." I sobbed.

"What did he do? Did he hurt you?"

"In the worst way possible."

Donovan came out of the bedroom and knelt down beside me, placing his hand on my arm.

"Come on. Let's get you to your room."

They both helped me up and hung on to me as they led me down the hall to my bedroom.

"Talk to me, Gabby. Tell me what he did. Do I need to call the police?"

I shook my head. "He didn't physically hurt me."

I tried to explain what happened, but I wasn't so sure how much they could understand because I was hysterical. I grabbed G by the shirt and looked at her. My eyes opened wide.

"G, I have to stop the pain. Please, just this once. I have to stop it. It hurts so bad."

"Gabby, no. You need to stay strong. You can't substitute one pain for another. You know that."

"Please, G, please." I had lost all control as I gripped her arms as tight as I could. "You don't know what it's like. You could never understand. I'm numb."

"Listen to me!" she yelled as she lightly shook me. "You're going to wait. Okay. Fifteen minutes, Gabby. Just fifteen minutes."

Donovan walked back into the room and placed something in her hand.

"Gabby, take this." She held up a small blue pill. "It's a Valium, and right now, you need it. Take this, and we'll wait fifteen minutes. After fifteen minutes, if you still feel the urge, then you can make yourself feel better. Okay?" She slowly nodded her head.

"Okay. Fifteen minutes," I said with tears streaming down my face. I took the pill from her, popped it in my mouth, and took a sip of water. It wasn't too long before it started to take effect. I fell asleep.

Chapter Twenty-Nine

I awoke to the faint sound of voices. My eyes were swollen shut, and my head was pounding like I was severely hung over.

"Giana, please. Just let me talk to her. I need to see for myself if she's okay."

"She's not okay, Simon. I've never seen her like this. I don't know all the details of what happened because she was hysterical last night. I just can't—"

"I know, and I'm sorry. Please just tell her I stopped by."

"I will."

I heard the door shut and opened my eyes. As I glanced over at the clock on the nightstand, I noticed it was one o'clock in the afternoon. I climbed out of bed and went into the bathroom. A look of horror swept across my face as I looked at myself in the mirror. My eyes were red and puffy, and my hair was messy. I splashed some cold water on my face and walked into the kitchen, where I saw Giana and Donovan sitting at the table, eating lunch.

"Hey, Gabs," G said.

"Hey." I heated some water for tea and grabbed a tea bag from the cupboard. "Why was he here?"

"You heard?"

"Yeah. It woke me up."

"I'm sorry. He's worried about you. He wanted to talk to you."

"There's nothing to talk about. The damage is done, and it's over." I poured the hot water in the cup and took it over to the table.

Donovan reached over and placed his hand on mine. "From a guy's point of view, he's hurting just as badly."

"Good. I hope he suffers for the rest of his damn life. He bought me, G. I was a fucking business deal."

"I know, and what he did wasn't right. But, Gabby, you need to stop and think about why he did it."

I put my hand up. "If you even think about defending his actions, either one of you, this friendship is over!" I shouted and went to the bathroom.

"We aren't defending him."

I turned on the water for a shower and noticed my razor was missing from the shelf.

"Where's my razor?" I asked as I stormed into the kitchen. Neither one said anything.

I opened the silverware drawer, and all the knives were missing. I turned and looked at the butcher block that we kept in the corner with the sharp knives and scissors in it, and it was gone.

"What the fuck are you doing?" I yelled.

"I wasn't taking any chances," G said in a raised voice as she got up from her chair. "You're very vulnerable right now and in a very bad place. I'm protecting you because I'll be fucking damned if I let you go down that road again!"

"I need to shave my legs, G! Please." I began to cry.

She walked over and hugged me. "I'm sorry he did this to you, but I can't until I know you're okay."

"I said things last night that I didn't mean. It was in the moment. I'll make you a deal: you give me my razor back so I can shave, and I'll show you when I get out of the shower that nothing happened. Please, G. I promise you, and I've never broken a promise. You, of all people, know that."

"Give it back to her, Giana," Donovan spoke.

She sighed. "Fine. Go take your shower, and I'll bring it to you."

I hugged her tight and then stepped into the shower, letting the hot water soak my body. A few moments later, Giana stuck her hand through the curtain.

"Here."

"Thank you."

I took the razor and set it down so I could lather my legs with shaving cream. I shaved like I said I would and set the razor on the shelf. I stepped out of the shower, put on new pajamas, and climbed back into bed. I stayed there for the next three days. Giana and Donovan took turns bringing me meals that I barely ate.

There was a light knock on my bedroom door, and when G opened it, she walked in holding a dozen red roses that were arranged in a beautiful crystal vase with baby's breath.

"Look what was just delivered for you."

I knew who they were from, and I didn't want them. "I don't want them."

"They're beautiful, Gabs. I'm going to set them on your dresser."

She gave me a small smile and walked out of the room. I could see a small white envelope amongst the roses from a distance. Curiosity got the best of me as I climbed out of bed and opened it.

>
> *Gabrielle,*
> *I love you, and I'm sorry.*
> *Forever my love, Simon*

I tore up the card and threw it in the trashcan. He could say "sorry" all he wanted to, but the damage was done. He had broken me beyond repair. I climbed back into bed and stayed there for another couple of days.

~

Two weeks had passed since that day in New York. Simon sent me a dozen roses with the same card every day, and the roses were a different color. I heard my phone beep with a text message from Katie.

"Hi. I was hoping you'd meet me for lunch today. It's a beautiful day out, and I thought maybe we could meet in the park. Work has totally sucked since you quit, and I would like to see you."

I climbed out of bed, opened my blinds, and stared out at the bright, sunny day for the first time in two weeks. Maybe it was time I stepped outside my pity zone and tried to reclaim my life.

"Hi. I would love to meet you for lunch."

"Great, Gabby. I miss you. Let's meet in the park at twelve-thirty. I'll bring lunch."

"Sounds good. I'll see you then."

I showered and put on a pair of beige Capri pants and a black short-sleeved shirt. The little snug pants not so long ago were now practically falling off. I grabbed my purse and my keys and drove to the park. This car was no longer mine, and I had to figure out how to return it.

"Hey." Katie smiled as she stood up and gave me a hug.

She had a blanket spread across the grass with a wicker picnic basket on top.

"It's good to see you, Katie."

I sat down on the blanket across from her as she reached into the basket and pulled out a couple of salads.

"I've been meaning to call, but I just didn't know what to say," she spoke.

"It's okay. I spent the last two weeks in bed."

"I hate that you're not my boss any more. Simon is a mess. He's irritable, and he's been yelling a lot. Every time he walks past your office, he stops and looks in. He's really broken up, Gabby."

"It's his own fault."

"I don't know what happened and it's none of my business, but maybe the two of you can work it out in time."

"No. I never want to see him again."

We sat and talked for a good two hours about life. She reached into her purse and handed me a card with the name of a doctor on it.

"This is Dr. Roberts' card. He used to be my therapist, and he's really good. He helped me a lot when I needed it, and I think he can help you too. Give him a call and try him out."

I held the small white business card in my hand and stared at it. Maybe it was time I talked to someone about my life.

"Thank you, Katie." We hugged goodbye, and I climbed into my car. I needed to get my life together, and the first thing I needed to do was to find a new job and get a new apartment. I pulled my phone from my purse and noticed a text message from Simon.

The Secret He Holds

"I know I'm the last person you want to hear from, but I miss you terribly. Again, I'm so sorry. Please, let's talk."

I deleted his message and made an appointment to see Dr. Roberts the day after tomorrow.

Chapter Thirty

"Have a seat, Gabrielle." Dr. Roberts smiled as he sat down in the chair across from me. I looked around at the pictures he had hanging on his white-painted walls. His wood-framed doctorate degree hung in the middle of his neatly arranged family photos.

"I was reviewing the questions you answered, and you've had a rough life. Why don't you start by telling me why you're here today."

"I don't really know," I softly spoke as I picked at my fingernails. "I was in a bad relationship for six years, and now I just ended one with a man who I truly loved because of something he did."

We sat and talked for an hour, and before I knew it, my time was up.

"I think it would be best if you saw me at least three times a week to start. You have some really deep issues that we need to try and fix."

"Thank you, Dr. Roberts. That won't be a problem since I don't have a job."

"Meanwhile, I want you to start taking the baby steps

necessary to build your life back up. I have an opening the day after tomorrow at nine o'clock."

"Sounds good. Thank you, Dr. Roberts."

When I arrived back at the apartment, Giana and Donovan were home from work and cooking dinner together in the kitchen.

"How did your appointment go?" G asked.

"It went well. I got a job." I smiled.

"You did? Where?"

"At the coffee shop down the street. It's only part-time because one of the girls is on maternity leave. But it's a start."

"Congratulations," Donovan said.

"Can I ask you guys for a favor?"

"Sure, Gabs. Anything."

"Can you follow me to Young International so I can drop off the car? Since I no longer work there, I can't keep it."

"Of course we can. We'll go right after dinner."

"There's something we should tell you," Donovan spoke. "Giana and I were having lunch down by the waterfront today, and we saw Simon. He looked pretty bad."

"Did you talk to him?"

"Yes. But it was just small talk. He asked how you were and told us he missed you."

"He sent me a text message today, telling me again that he was sorry and that he loves me. I can't…I just can't." I left the kitchen and walked to my room.

∽

At six a.m., I put on my running clothes and headed to the waterfront. It was lightly raining, so I pulled my hood up on my hoody as I ran along the path. I had to be training at the coffee shop at ten, so I didn't want to run too long. My mind was racing with things I didn't want to think about, and I couldn't concentrate on anything else since I had left my iPod at home. I looked down to see that my damn shoe was untied. I either had to get new laces or buy new shoes. I stopped by a bench and bent down as I propped my foot on it so I could tie it. I froze when I heard his voice.

"Gabrielle."

My heart began to race, and my stomach instantly knotted. I slowly turned around and looked at the man who destroyed me for the first time since that day. His desolate eyes locked onto mine. He looked horrible. His face looked heavy, and it looked as if he hadn't shaven in days. His eyes stared straight into my soul and pleaded with me to say something.

"I have to go."

"Please, don't. Let me look at you a little longer."

His voice was no longer controlled, and the once poised and confident man I had grown to love was gone.

"I can't. I have to go. Please leave me alone. If you love me like you say you do, you'll leave me alone."

"We need to talk, Gabrielle."

"There are no more words, Simon. What's done is done. Now, if you'll excuse me, I have to go."

I needed to run from him as fast as I could. It killed me to see him that way, but he did it to himself. I ran all the way home, showered, and changed for my first day at the coffee shop.

∼

The Secret He Holds

"Before we can let you start making the coffee beverages, you need to memorize each drink. So here's the training booklet for you to look over. You can also take it home with you," Lorraine, my manager, said. "You can take a seat at that table if you like and start to read it over. Try to become familiar with each beverage."

I smiled and took the manual over to the table and scanned it. After about fifteen minutes, I got up and walked over to Lorraine, handing her the manual.

"Why are you giving this back?" she asked with a confused look.

"I'm done reading it."

She laughed. "You aren't taking this seriously, are you?"

"I am, and I've read it."

"Okay, Miss Smarty Pants. Let's put you to the test."

Lorraine rattled off a number of different lattes and specialty coffees for me to make. I made each one perfectly as she stood there in shock.

"Okay then. Care to explain how you did that?"

"I have a photographic memory."

"Oh. Well, I guess you do. I think you're going to do just fine here." She smiled.

I finished my shift and was pleased at how well I did. Since the coffee shop was only a couple of blocks away, I could easily walk home. As I approached my apartment building, I noticed the company car Simon had given me was parked in a parking spot. I stood there in disbelief and noticed a note sticking up from the windshield wiper.

"This car is yours. It was always yours to keep, no matter what."

I took the note and went up to my apartment. I threw

my purse down and called for G. No one was home. I grabbed my phone and sent a text message to Simon.

"I'm not keeping the car."

"Then sell it. I told you it's yours."

Just as I was about to slam down my phone, the door opened, and G and Donovan walked in.

"What's wrong? You have that look. And by the way, how did your old car get back here?"

"Simon left this note on it," I said as I practically threw it at her.

"Oh. Well then, it's yours. Accept it and move on. Now you won't have to go and buy one."

"That's not the point." I scowled.

"He's trying to make up, Gabby," Donovan spoke.

"He can try all he wants. Me, him, and us will never happen again."

~

It was eight thirty the next morning, and I needed to get to Dr. Roberts's office. I was running late because I overslept. I grabbed the keys to the car and drove to my appointment. If I decided to keep the car, then Simon would think I was softening up towards him, and that wasn't the case. I would just be borrowing it until I found another.

"Good morning, Gabrielle." Dr. Roberts smiled as he called me into his office. "How are you doing?"

"I'm okay," I said as I took a seat in the same comfy chair as last time. "I got a job."

"Fantastic. Step one is making a change for the better. That was quick."

I smiled. "It's only at a coffee shop by my apartment. It isn't my dream job, but it'll do for now."

"Have you heard from Simon?"

I looked down. "Yes. He sent me a text message apologizing again and telling me that he loved me. He also gave me back the car I returned."

"Why do you suppose he did that?"

"To try and weaken me so he can walk back into my life as if nothing happened."

Dr. Roberts crossed his legs and narrowed his eyes at me. "I'm familiar with Simon Young, by what I've read about him in the newspapers. He's never been with the same woman for more than a week. His telling you that he loves you isn't a game to him. I believe he does, but that's not the point here. The point is that you don't because he's hurt you so deeply."

"I was nothing but a business deal to him and Brendon."

"Let's talk about Brendon for a moment. You told me that he verbally and emotionally abused you for six years. You believed he truly loved you, so no matter how mean and vile he was, you wouldn't leave him because you so desperately wanted to be loved. Which was something you never felt growing up."

"True, and I've learned from my mistakes. I will never fall into that kind of trap again."

"Tell me something. Tell me when you were the happiest and at peace with your life."

I shifted in my chair because it wasn't hard to answer, and it rolled off my tongue before I could stop it.

"When I was with Simon."

"Interesting. So out of your entire twenty-four years of life, your happiest and most peaceful time was when you were with him?"

"That was before I knew I was nothing but a business deal," I spewed.

The bell rang, alerting us that our time was up. "Gabrielle, I want you to take something into consideration."

"What?" I asked as I got up from my seat.

"I would like Mr. Young to join one of our sessions."

My mouth dropped. "What? No way!"

"I think it would be beneficial in helping you. I would like to hear the reasoning behind his actions. Give it some thought. Don't rule it out just yet. I'll see you in a couple of days."

I walked out of his office and climbed into my car. There was no way Simon was getting involved in my therapy sessions.

Chapter Thirty-One

Another week had passed. My job was going well, and I continued my therapy sessions with Dr. Roberts. Donovan's wife was found competent to stand trial, so it was going to be a grueling next few months for him and G. I hadn't heard from Simon since he dropped off the car. Was I happy about that? I didn't know. Simon Young wasn't a man that was easy to forget.

I was working at the coffee shop, taking a drink order, when I looked up and saw Simon standing in line. My body instantly tightened, and my heart started to race. When it was his turn, he smiled as he stepped up to the counter.

"Hi, Gabrielle."

The sight of him should have sickened me, but it didn't. He was clean-shaven, his hair was perfectly in place, and he was in his dark grey expensive designer suit.

"What can I get you?" I said as I looked down.

"What kind of tea do you recommend?"

"Depends on what you like."

"I think you already know what I like."

I looked up at him as I bit down on my lip. My palms were sweaty, and I felt like I was losing control.

"I recommend the chai tea with soy milk. It's really good."

Lorraine stood to the side of me, watching the two of us.

"That sounds good. I'll have one of those." He reached in his pocket and pulled out a wad of cash.

I took the money from him, and he closed his hand on mine when I gave him his change. I couldn't pull away. It was only for a second, but it felt like he was never letting go. Lorraine handed him his cup, and he smiled and thanked her.

"I'll see you around," he said before walking out.

I looked over at Lorraine, who was staring at the door. "Do you know who that was? I think he was flirting with you."

"Yeah, I know him. I used to work for him."

Her eyes widened. "What? That wasn't on your application."

"It's a job I want to forget ever existed."

"Damn. If I worked for that sexy man, I'd never quit."

I looked at her and gave her a small smile. My shift had ended, so I grabbed my purse and noticed it was raining when I stepped out the door. Shit. I didn't bring an umbrella. It wasn't a mere mist but a steady rain that soaked me as I walked home. When I approached the building, I stopped dead in my tracks when I saw Simon sitting on one of the benches outside. It reminded me of the time we sat on the bench outside my old building, where he confessed his love for tea.

"What are you doing here? It's raining, and you're soaked."

He looked up at me as his arms rested on his legs. "I

don't know. I guess I wanted to make sure you got home okay."

"Are you stalking me or something? Because I swear to God, Simon."

"If making sure you're okay and that you arrived home safely is stalking you, then I guess I am."

I sighed and sat down next to him. "You need to stop, Simon. I can't deal with it. I hadn't heard from you in over a week, and I thought that was it. I thought you'd moved on."

"I was giving you space," he spoke as he turned his head and looked at me. "I'm a monster, and I don't deserve to be liked by someone like you or anyone at all. What I did, I did for the right reasons, but the wrong way. I know my apologies are never going to be enough, and I don't blame you for hating me. I hate myself. I'm only here to ask you for one thing and one thing only, and then I'll never bother you again. I promise."

I closed my eyes as the rain fell down on us. "What?"

"I'm asking for your forgiveness because I can't live the rest of my life knowing that you hate me."

At that moment, and for the first time since New York, I felt calm.

"I can't do that just yet, Simon, and you need to understand that." I got up and walked towards the door. I stopped before my hand could reach the knob and looked at him as he lowered his head. "Come inside, and I'll get you a towel to dry off. You're going to catch pneumonia."

He turned his head and looked at me as he slowly got up from the bench and followed me inside the apartment. I ran to the bathroom and grabbed two towels. "Here. Dry yourself off." I patted my face and then ran the towel through my soaking wet hair.

"Do you like working at the coffee shop?" he asked.

"Yeah. I do."

"I'm happy to hear that."

Suddenly, the door opened, and G walked in.

"Oh," she said in surprise. "Hi, Simon." She gave me an odd look.

"Hello, Giana. How are you?"

"I'm okay. How are you?"

"I'm okay."

"Good to hear," she said as she walked past him.

"I read in the papers that Donovan's wife will stand trial."

"Yeah. There's no way anyone will find her innocent. That bitch is going to prison."

"I hope she does for what she did. I better get going." He handed me the towel. "Thanks, Gabrielle, for the towel. Have a good night." He walked out the door.

After a few moments of pondering, I ran out after him. Before he reached the building door, I called his name.

"Simon, wait."

He turned around and stared at me.

I swallowed hard. "I'm seeing a therapist. His name is Dr. Roberts, and we've been talking about you. He thinks that it would be a good idea for you to join me in a session. That's only if you want to, of course."

"Of course. If it'll help you."

"Okay. I have an appointment tomorrow night at six o'clock. I'll text you the address."

"I'll be there. Have a good night, Gabrielle."

"You too." He walked out the door and was gone. I stood there and let out a deep breath.

I went back up to the apartment, and G was waiting at the door. "Well, what was all that about?" she asked.

"I told him that Dr. Roberts wanted him to sit in on a session, and he said he would."

"Of course he did. He's trying to get you back. He's going to do anything you ask."

I put up my hand and went to the kitchen for a glass of wine. "He told me today that he'd leave me alone for good if I only did one thing."

"What does he want?"

"He wants me to forgive him. He said he can't live the rest of his life knowing I hate him."

"Fuck, Gabby. The man is in love with you and is trying to make amends. People do fucked up and crazy things." She cleared her throat and looked down at my arm.

"Oh my God, G, how could you?" I picked up the glass and took it over to the couch.

"It's the truth. Listen, Gabs, if it was only a business deal, then he wouldn't be going to all this trouble to get you back or ask for forgiveness. If the man didn't love or care for you, he would write it off as a bad business deal. But that's not what he's doing."

"Can we please talk about something else? I'm done with the subject of Simon Young."

My stomach knotted as I pulled into the parking lot of Dr. Roberts' office. I was about fifteen minutes early, so I got out of my car, went into the building, and took my usual seat in the waiting room, waiting for Simon to walk through the door. Maybe he wouldn't show. I couldn't imagine that therapists were his thing. At about five-fifty-five, the door opened, and Simon walked in. He smiled and took the seat next to me.

"Hi," he said in a low voice.

"Hi." I looked down.

Dr. Roberts opened his office door and broke the awkward silence between us. "Gabrielle, come on in."

"Hi, Dr. Roberts. This is Simon Young."

"Hello, Simon. Nice to meet you."

"Likewise, Dr. Roberts."

"Please have a seat." He motioned us over to the couch.

"Can I get you two anything to drink?"

"I'm good. Thank you," Simon replied.

"Do you have any strong alcohol around here?"

Dr. Roberts smiled. "Sorry, Gabrielle. All I have is water, coffee, juice, or tea."

"Then I'm fine," I said as I put up my hand.

Dr. Roberts grabbed his notepad before sitting down across from us. He pushed up his glasses, which sat low on the bridge of his nose.

"Simon, thank you for coming tonight. Tell me why you agreed to come."

Simon shifted his body and crossed his legs. "I came for Gabrielle. I need to make her see how sorry I am for what happened."

"Do you think she believes you?" he asked.

"No."

Dr. Roberts looked at me. "Gabby? Do you believe he's sorry for what happened?"

I inhaled deeply. "I don't know. I don't know what to believe anymore. Anything in my life that seems real turns out to be fake," I spoke as I wiped a tear that was about to fall.

Simon reached over to me.

"Don't touch me," I snapped.

"Why are you so angry, Gabby?" Dr. Roberts asked.

"Because of what he did to me."

"How did he make you feel?"

"Like a fucking whore. A million-dollar whore!" The tears were starting to fall faster than I could stop them. I grabbed a tissue from the table next to the couch. "I was a part of his plan. He used the one thing that he knew would destroy me to his advantage."

"Brendon?" Dr. Roberts asked as he held up his pen.

"Yes!"

"Simon, would you like to comment?"

"Gabrielle, I'm sorry. You're right about using Brendon, but he was no good for you. My god, the sadness in your eyes when I first saw you on the plane was like nothing I'd ever seen before. You were trying so hard to get his approval, and he dismissed you like you were nothing. For fuck's sake, he stopped you from eating a chocolate bar. He wouldn't have sex with you, and when he did, the lights had to be turned off. He was constantly putting you down and comparing you to other women. You didn't deserve that. I wanted to save you right then and there on the plane. I wanted to grab you and take you away from him. When you turned around and looked at me as I helped you with your bag, I was hooked, and you have been on my mind ever since. I would lie in bed at night and wonder if he was mistreating you. Knowing that you were with someone like him burned me to my core. I knew your life would be better if you came to Seattle and worked for me. I knew you'd be safe. I needed to get you away from him. I guess I was falling in love with you already. Brendon gave you up without a fight. Why can't you see that?"

"He's always been a piece of shit! It doesn't surprise me, Simon. Why couldn't you have just come to New York and try to be friends with me? Arranged a coincidental meeting?"

"Would you have met with me somewhere?" he asked.

"Yes, because I had thought about you every single day since that flight. I never forgot you," I cried.

Simon lowered his head. "I'm so sorry."

"Look at me," I commanded. "The only thing I ever wanted in my whole entire life was to be loved by someone. Was that so much to ask for? Isn't everyone loved by someone in their lifetime? My need to be loved drove me to cut. The emotional pain of being a complete nobody took over my life. Then Brendon came along, and I still cut because I knew deep down he didn't love me, but I kept telling myself over and over that he did."

Simon stared at me with tears in his eyes. "Have you cut because of me?"

"No."

"Thank God." He sighed.

"Don't think I haven't thought about it, because I have."

"Gabrielle, if I could go back in time and erase the past, I would. But I wouldn't erase the moment I saw you on that plane."

I sat there in silence, taking in everything he said and drying my eyes.

"Gabby, do you have anything else to say?" Dr. Roberts asked.

I shook my head, and the bell rang. "Our time is up here." He thanked Simon for coming, and the two of us walked out of his office. Simon's car was parked next to mine.

"Thanks for coming." I walked to my car, and Simon called out to me as I opened the door.

"I meant every word, Gabrielle. Every single word."

I nodded, climbed into my car, and drove home.

Chapter Thirty-Two

I spent the last week thinking about Simon and that session. The words he spoke, the tears in his eyes, and the sincerity in his voice. Dr. Roberts told me that we live in an imperfect world with imperfect people. People are allowed to make mistakes because that's how we learn and grow. I was far from perfect. Cutting myself to ease my emotional pain was a mistake I had made. Simon made a mistake thinking that he could have me by turning me into a business deal. I made peace with my cutting and with myself, and Simon deserved the same. It was seven o'clock, and I was hungry. I picked up my phone and dialed Simon. He immediately answered.

"Gabrielle."

"Hi. We need to talk."

"Name a time and place."

"In about fifteen minutes, at the café next to the coffee shop."

"I'll be there."

I ended the call and walked to the kitchen, where G and Donovan were eating pizza.

"Are you sure you don't want a slice?" she asked.

"Nah. I'm going to meet Simon over at the diner by the coffee shop."

"Good girl. Have fun." She smiled.

Donovan was in the middle of chewing and gave me a thumbs-up. I grabbed my purse and walked to the diner.

When I walked in, I took a booth in the corner, where it was quiet and away from the few people that were in the place. A few moments later, Simon walked in, and I raised my hand so he would see me. He looked so damn good in his khaki pants and white cotton button-up shirt. He sat down across from me, and I could tell he was nervous.

"Hi." He smiled.

"Hi."

Before I could say another word, the waitress walked over, handed us our menus, and took our drink order.

"You said you wanted to talk."

"I've been thinking a lot over the past week, and I wanted to tell you that I forgive you."

"You do? Really?" he asked to be certain.

"Yes. Nobody's perfect, and we all make mistakes. You did save me, Simon. You saved me from living in a non-existent relationship and living a life of misery. My mistake was that I jumped into things with you way too fast after Brendon. I didn't get a chance to be alone and explore my life as an adult. I grew up way too fast. I depended on the first boy who looked my way to care for me, but I ended up caring for him. I want to be your friend, Simon, and that's all I can be. It's going to take a long time for me to be able to trust anyone again."

He sat there, his beautiful, sad eyes staring directly at me, soaking up every word I said.

"I understand, Gabrielle, and I'll take your friendship

because having you in my life as a friend is better than not having you at all."

I reached across the table and placed my hand on his. "Thank you, Simon."

We ordered some food and talked a bit about Young International and the coffee shop. As soon as we were finished, we walked outside the diner.

"Did you walk?" he asked.

"Yeah."

"Would it be okay if I walked you home so that I know you arrived safely?"

"I think it would be okay if you drove me home." I smiled.

"My car is this way." He motioned with his hand and a smile.

As he pulled up to the curb, and before I got out, I turned and looked at him.

"Thank you for the ride, friend. And, for the record, you're not a monster."

"You're welcome, friend. Thank you. I appreciate that."

∼

A month had passed, and I would occasionally see Simon down by the waterfront when I went running. We would see each other from a distance and wave like any friend would do. He sometimes stopped by the coffee house to pick up a chai tea, and we would send an occasional text message here and there. The trial was finally over, and Sylvia was found guilty of attempted murder in the first degree. Needless to say, she would be spending the rest of her life in prison. Donovan proposed to Giana, and she said yes. It was going to be time for me to find a new place to live. I still saw Dr. Roberts, but only one day a week.

It was a Wednesday, and Simon had stopped by the coffee house.

"Hi, Gabrielle."

"Hi. I'm glad you stopped in. I'm just going on break. Do you have a few minutes?"

"Of course."

"Great. Go sit down, and I'll bring us two chai teas."

I made the drinks and took them over to the table. He politely thanked me as I sat down.

"I'm throwing an engagement party for Giana and Donovan, and I wanted to invite you. That is, if you'd like to come." I smiled.

"I'd love to. When is it?"

"I don't know yet. I'm still trying to find a place to have it. The apartment is too small, but I placed a call to that restaurant, The Rooftop, to see if they could accommodate us for next Saturday, but they haven't gotten back to me yet."

"Have the party at my place," he spoke.

"That's nice of you, but no. I couldn't."

"Why not? I have more than enough room, especially in the backyard. They're my friends too. Let me do this for them. You still plan everything. I have a great event coordinator who will work with you if you're interested."

"Really? You're serious?"

"Of course I am. It'll be fun. Her name is Sabrina, and I've used her for years. She's good. I'll give her a call and have her call you."

"Thank you, Simon."

"You're welcome, Gabrielle. Now I need to run. I have a meeting to get to." He smiled as he winked at me.

Shit. That look. That wink. That smile. I crossed my legs because the Simon ache was back with a vengeance.

Chapter Thirty-Three

I pulled up to the gates that sat in front of Simon's house and alerted his staff I was there. When I pulled up, Sabrina got out of her car.

"Gabrielle, it's so nice to meet you."

"Thank you. It's nice to meet you, too. Thank you for helping me out."

"Oh, please. When Simon calls, I drop everything." She laughed.

She was beautiful with long, straight black hair that looked like silk and jade-colored eyes. My mind couldn't help but wonder if Simon had ever fucked her. We walked through the house and to the backyard. We sat down at the table, and Sabrina summoned over one of Simon's maids.

"Could you please bring us a couple of cosmopolitans?" she asked.

"Coming right up, Miss Sabrina."

"If we're going to plan a party, we might as well get our drink on while we do it." She winked. "Since it's for an engagement, I think we should do a 'white' party. White tents, lights, tablecloths, candles, and perhaps even a few swans to swim in the pool."

"All that sounds amazing, but I think it may be a bit out of my budget."

"Oh, please," she said with a wave of her hand. "The entire party is on Simon. He told me to spare no expense."

"What?" I pulled out my phone.

"There is no way I'm letting you pay for the party."

I set down my phone and waited for his reply as a cosmopolitan was set down in front of me.

"Also, all the guests have to wear white. How many people were you thinking?"

"Seventy people."

She nodded her head. "Okay, that's a decent size. I can work with that number on such short notice."

I picked up my drink and took a sip just as Simon walked in. "Well, hello, you two. Party planning, I see."

"Hello, Simon darling."

"She wants swans." I smiled.

Simon looked at me and narrowed his eyes. "Swans, eh? In my pool?"

"Oh, shush, Simon. It'll be amazing. Now follow me around the yard, and I'll show you what I'm planning."

We followed Sabrina around the yard as she waved her hands around and pointed to where the tents would be placed.

"Did you get my text message?" I asked Simon.

"I did, and it's not up for discussion, Gabrielle. I told you I was taking care of this."

"No, you didn't. You said I could use your house."

"That's right, and when events are held at my house, I pay for them. So, if we're done here, I'm going to go upstairs and change." He walked away with a smile on his face.

Sabrina walked over to me with a pointed finger. "Nobody tells Simon no." She smiled.

I sighed and sat back at the table as we picked out the invitations. "That should be it for now. The invitations will be ready in a couple of days, so get me the guest list and the addresses, and I'll take care of the mailing. Don't worry, Gabrielle. I will take care of the rest. All you need to do is show up in a fabulous white dress." She finished her drink, kissed me on the cheek, and left.

I couldn't help but wonder if Simon had slept with her. Just the way she talked about him led me to believe he did, and I was very uncomfortable with it. As I sat at the table, Simon walked back to the patio and sat down across from me.

"Did you fuck her?" The words fell out of my mouth without warning.

"Why would you ask me that?"

"Why not? Just the way she talked about you led me to believe you did."

"I can assure you I never have. It would be pretty hard since she's not into men."

"Oh." I felt like an ass.

"Would you like another drink?"

"No. I need to get going. I have to pack."

"Pack? Are you going somewhere?"

"G, a friend of hers from the law firm, and I are having a girls' weekend getaway."

"Sounds nice. Where are you going?"

"Somewhere." I smiled.

"Ah, so it's a secret."

"Yeah. Donovan doesn't even know. It's just for us girls to get away, be pampered, and relax."

"Sounds great. I hope you have a good time, Gabrielle."

"Thanks, Simon. I'll talk to you when I get back."

"Be safe," he said as he gave me a concerned look.

"I will." I placed my hand on his shoulder as I walked past him.

~

The three of us boarded the plane and took our seats. Lana, G's friend from the firm, was super sweet and funny. She was thirty years old and newly divorced, so this weekend getaway was to celebrate, and, according to her, what better way to celebrate a divorce than Vegas! I really didn't want to go because of the memories Vegas held for me. G told me to forget about them, drink, and have a good time. I wasn't so sure. As G and I talked, Lana looked at me and showed me a picture on her iPad.

"Gabby, don't you know Simon Young?" She handed me her iPad, and there was a picture of him from last night with a beautiful brunette hanging on his arm. It was taken at an event for breast cancer awareness. She wore a beautiful, long, pink, shimmery gown, and he was in a black tuxedo with a light pink bowtie. I swallowed hard as I answered her.

"Yeah, he's a friend," I spoke as I handed her the iPad.

G placed her hand on my arm. "Are you okay?" she asked in a whisper.

"Of course I'm okay. Why wouldn't I be?"

"Well, you know," she pouted.

"We're friends, G, and nothing else. You know that. I would be stupid as fuck to think that he wasn't seeing other women."

"You saw him yesterday. He didn't mention he was going out?"

"Why would he? He doesn't owe me any explanation as to where he goes. Just like I don't owe him any."

"Alright. Remember, we're going to Vegas, baby. Hot guys, plenty of booze, and for you, cards." She winked.

I gave her a small smile as I looked out the window of the plane. I brought my knees up to my chest and thought about Simon. Seeing him with that woman stirred up jealousy I shouldn't have had. The plane landed, and once again, I was in Vegas. A place that I didn't even like but kept being brought back to by different people.

"What hotel are we staying at?" I asked Lana.

"I booked us a room at the Hard Rock."

When the cab dropped us off at the curb, I looked down the strip at Simon's hotel. The very one where we first made love to each other. As G and I stayed back while Lana went up to the desk, we wondered why it was taking her so long to check-in.

"What's taking so long?" G asked her.

"These fucking idiots double-booked our room, and they don't have another room available. So they're calling around to see what they can find us at a different hotel."

After a few moments, the reservation clerk came back and apologized. She told us we were put into a suite at the Emerald Hotel and Casino. I instantly felt sick.

"Jackpot! Not only do we get to stay in one of the most luxurious hotels in Vegas, but we get a suite, and the Hard Rock is taking care of the additional expense!" she exclaimed. "This trip is getting better and better."

G looked at me. "What's wrong, Gabby?"

"That's Simon's hotel."

"The same one you stayed at with him?"

"Yep."

She hooked her arm around me. "It'll be okay. I promise."

We took our bags and walked down to the hotel. Memories of our stay here invaded my mind the minute I stepped in. After getting settled in our suite, we put on our bathing suits, went down to the pool, and drank one too many cocktails. Later that night, I went down to the casino and played some cards while G and Lana pulled some slots and went back to the room with a substantial amount of money.

~

The next morning, the three of us had spa appointments. We bathed in mud, had our bodies wrapped in cellophane, and then had the most amazing massages by the hottest guys in the hotel. I couldn't get that picture of Simon out of my mind, and it saddened me. I didn't even want to think about him with her and the things they did, but I couldn't help it. Later that day, we did some shopping, and then I went back down to the casino by myself while they went to a show. I told them I wasn't feeling well from drinking all day, so I was just going to stay back in the room. I hit the blackjack table first and was careful. But as the waitress kept coming by with drinks, I would have one, and as soon as that was gone, I'd grab another. Before I knew it, I was flying high and moving from table to table, winning and winning big. All my rules were now consumed by alcohol, and I knew I was being watched. *Get a grip, Gabby. Slow down.* Before I knew it, I had a crowd around me at the poker table, up to almost fifty thousand dollars. The drinks kept coming, and I kept drinking, trying to drown my sorrows. A man came up to me and asked me if I was interested in playing in the high roller room. I knew that was their trick to get their money back.

"No, I'm good." I smiled.

He left, and I continued to win, with a crowd cheering me on. As I sipped my martini, a man in a security uniform walked up to me and lightly took hold of my arm.

"Ma'am, you need to come with me, please."

Shit. Shit. Shit. I got caught.

He took me into a room where two other men and a woman stood up against a window.

"Have a seat, please."

"What's this about? Is this how you treat all your guests?"

"Only the ones who we suspect of counting cards," he said smugly.

"Don't be ridiculous," I said, waving my hand at them.

"Care to explain how you won all that money? This isn't the first night either. We were watching you last night as well."

"It's called luck of the draw, fellas and ma'am. People don't come in here and win big? Isn't that what casinos are for?"

"You've won over $50,000 tonight alone and $20,000 last night. Had you stayed out of the casino tonight, we wouldn't have thought about it."

"You're being ridiculous. Now, if you'll excuse me, I'm not feeling well."

"Sorry, ma'am, but we can't let you leave yet."

"What are you going to do? Call the police? Because the last time I checked, counting cards wasn't illegal. So all you need to do is ban me from this hotel, and I'll be on my way," I said as I got up from the chair.

"No, it's not illegal, but it is my hotel," I heard Simon's voice say as he entered the room.

My heart stopped as I turned around and saw him smiling at me.

"Thank you for holding her. You're free to go. I can take it from here."

He walked around to the chair and placed his hands on the arms, bending over so his face was inches from mine. "Having fun on your girls' getaway?"

"I was until your goons stopped me." I smiled. "Did you know I was here?"

"No. Not until I received a call a few hours ago from my security team, telling me that they recognized you from when we were here last, and you were winning an awful lot of money."

"Oh."

"What happened, Gabrielle? You broke your own rules."

"I'm blaming it on the alcohol I consumed."

He held out his hand and helped me up from my chair, placing his arm around my waist and staring into my eyes.

"I do believe this is the second time you've ripped off my casino."

"Third. But who's counting."

My heart was racing, and my palms were sweaty from his touch.

"Your palms are sweating. Are you excited or nervous?" he asked as his gaze took hold of me.

"I don't know," I whispered, as I could feel myself becoming highly aroused.

His eyes scanned my lips, and then he slowly closed them. He let go of me and turned away. "Enjoy the rest of your weekend with the girls," he said as he walked out of the room, leaving me there, feeling breathless.

The alcohol was still moving through my body, giving me the courage to do what I never would have done before. After a few moments, I left the room and went up to Simon's suite, praying he'd be there. Once the elevator reached the top floor and the doors opened, I lightly knocked on the door. When he opened it, I lunged at him, wrapped my arms around his neck, and smashed my mouth into his like a wild animal. He didn't push me away as he kissed me back and slipped his tongue deep into my mouth.

"Gabrielle," he said with bated breath.

"Just fuck me, Simon. Please," I begged as I lifted my sundress over my head.

He took in a sharp breath and pushed me up against the wall as I wrapped my legs around his waist, his hands having a firm grip on my ass as he held me up. Our tongues danced, and our lips couldn't get enough of each other. My hands tangled through his hair as his tongue slid down my neck and across my chest. He stopped, set me down, and undid his pants, taking them off and kicking them to the side. His fingers hooked around the waist of my panties and slid them off my hips while his tongue traveled down my torso and to my clit. He flicked it with his tongue and dipped his fingers inside me. I was already about to climax. He had me so hot and bothered, and it had been so long since he was inside of me. He came back up and lifted me so I would wrap my legs around him, thrusting in and out of me like a madman.

"Fuck, Gabrielle, I've missed you so bad." His breath hitched.

Tightening my arms around his neck, I let out a howl as he pushed deeper inside me, causing me to explode. He filled my insides with his come. His final thrust was deep and long as he moaned and buried his face into my neck. Our hearts were racing, and our bodies were sweating.

"Simon."

"Yes, baby," he said as he lifted his head and looked at me.

"I'm going to be sick." I unwrapped my legs from his waist and ran to the bathroom.

As I leaned over the toilet and threw up, Simon took my hair and held it with one hand while he rubbed my back with the other.

"Well, this is a first. No woman has ever thrown up after I've fucked her before."

I couldn't help but let out a laugh before throwing up again. When I finished, I sat on the bathroom floor while Simon gently wiped my mouth.

"I think you need to go lie down."

"Yeah, the room is sort of spinning at the moment."

He picked me up and carried me to the bed, gently laying me down. He walked over to his bag and pulled out a white T-shirt.

"Sit up for a minute so I can put this on you."

"I have to go back to my room. G will be worried about me."

"You're staying here?" he asked.

"Yeah. The Hard Rock double-booked our room."

"Why am I not surprised?" He smiled. "I'll call her right now and tell her what happened and that you'll be spending the night in my room."

"Thank you." I slowly closed my eyes as my head sank into the oversized comfy pillow.

Chapter Thirty-Four

Oh, my aching head. I put my hand on my head as I tried to open my eyes. I was lying flat on my back, and Simon had his arm tucked tightly around me as he slept on his side.

"Are you okay?"

"I'm not sure. My head feels like it's going to explode." I rolled over and snuggled against him, tucking my head into his chest. He kissed the top of my head as he lightly chuckled.

"I don't think it's very funny."

"That's what happens when you drink too much. But I must say, I really like drunk Gabrielle."

"I need coffee, like yesterday," I murmured in his chest.

"Then you're going to have to let me get up so I can get you some."

I sighed as I lifted my head and looked at him. His morning look was still as sexy as ever. He smiled as he kissed the tip of my nose, and I rolled over. He climbed out of bed and put on a pair of sweatpants. I stared at him as he strutted across the room and over to the desk where the hotel phone sat. Damn, his backside was amazing. It sent chills down my spine just looking at it.

"Good morning, Roberta. I need you to send up two coffees as soon as possible."

"I'm going to take a hot shower." I climbed out of bed and walked to the bathroom.

"Okay. I'll have two aspirin waiting for you when you get out."

I turned on the water and stepped in. As I tilted my head back and let the hot water run through my hair, I couldn't help but think about what had happened last night. I screwed one of my friends, and he was seeing someone else. I put my hands over my face. I needed to right this wrong. After showering, I put on the bathrobe hanging on the hook in the bathroom. Ugh, I hated these white robes. When I opened the door and walked into the main area of the suite, Simon was sitting at the table, looking over the newspaper.

"Feel better?"

"Sort of."

"Come sit down. I'll pour you some coffee."

As I sat down in the chair, Simon handed me some aspirin. "I got you a glass of orange juice."

"Thank you." I popped the pills in my mouth and took a sip of the juice. "About last night, Simon. I'm sorry."

"Sorry for what?"

"For coming up here. I never should have. It was a mistake. I was drunk and not thinking clearly."

He didn't say anything for a few moments. He just stared at me over the cup of coffee he was drinking.

"You're right, and I'm sorry that I followed through on what you asked me to do. I never should have, considering you'd been drinking."

I let out a sigh of relief. He thought it was a mistake

too. "It's totally my fault. I would just like to put it behind us."

"We're friends, Gabrielle, and sometimes sex happens. It's not the end of the world or our friendship. So if you're okay with what happened, then let's move on."

Why was he okay with it? Did he feel guilty for fucking me while he had that girl back in Seattle? God, the thought of him and her made my already sick stomach churn.

"Agreed. We're moving on." I faked a smile.

He looked down at the newspaper and I sat there and drank my coffee. "I was giving you the money, you know?"

"What do you mean?" His eyes looked up at me.

"The money I won last night. I was giving it back."

"No one does that, Gabrielle."

"I know, but it's your hotel, and I wouldn't have felt right. I didn't plan on winning so much. I got a little carried away."

"I would say for seventy thousand dollars, you went to the extreme. But keep it. I want you to have it. You won it, so it's yours."

"I won it by cheating. I'm not keeping it. If you don't take it, I'll turn it over to the casino manager."

"If you insist. It's your money." He shrugged.

"When are you leaving Vegas?"

"Probably today. There's no reason for me to stick around, and I have some stuff at home to do."

"You can hang with us?"

"Three girls and a guy. Actually, that would be any man's dream." He winked. "But you go and enjoy the rest of your trip. I'll see you when you get back to Seattle."

His aloof attitude bothered me. "Okay. Well, I'm going to head back to my room now," I said as I got up from the chair and picked up my clothes scattered on the floor. "Thanks again for last night."

"It was my pleasure, Gabrielle. I'll see you back in Seattle."

"Have a safe flight back." A small smile escaped my lips.

I pushed the elevator button and waited for the doors to open. I was hurting, and I shouldn't have been. My heart was breaking all over again because I missed him so much. It was my choice to be friends and end our relationship. He was now dating someone else, and I could never let what happened last night happen again.

We, or I should say they, enjoyed the rest of the trip, and I couldn't get home fast enough. I had to be back to work by ten Monday morning. Before leaving the hotel, I gave the money I won back to the casino manager, who also happened to be one of the men who held me until Simon arrived. He apologized to me but said he was following orders. I told him it was okay and that I understood. When I arrived home, I unpacked my suitcase and climbed into bed. Giana and Donovan had plenty of catching up to do. I was secretly wishing I could do some catching up with Simon. As I lay in bed, I pulled up the pictures of Simon and that beautiful woman. There were more pictures posted. One of them facing the camera, dancing, laughing, and sitting down at a table together with drinks in their hands. I was so ashamed for what I had done.

The next morning, I awoke at six o'clock and decided to go for a run before work. I put my earphones in my ears and ran down along the waterfront. My stomach did a flip when I saw Simon running towards me.

"Hey. How was your trip?" He was out of breath.

"It was good." I took one earphone from my ear.

"Good. Are you getting excited for the party this coming weekend?"

"Yeah. I am. It'll be great, and, by the way, I gave back the money."

"I know. Bart called and told me. Anyway, I need to get going. I'm meeting someone for breakfast."

"Okay. Enjoy, and it was good to see you," I said with a fake smile.

"Good seeing you too, Gabrielle. Have a good day." He jogged away, and I put my earphones back in and turned the volume on my music as my day was now completely ruined. He was happy, and I was miserable, and I had no one to blame except myself.

∼

"How did your girls' weekend go?" Dr. Roberts asked.

"Eventful. I slept with Simon."

"What? Did he go with you?"

"No. He was there on business and we ran into each other at the hotel." I lied, but I couldn't tell him what I did.

"And how do you feel?"

"Like shit. He has a girlfriend."

"Hmm…Did the two of you talk about it?"

"We both agreed it was a mistake and it won't happen again."

"Do you regret breaking things off with him?"

"I think so. I miss him. I miss seeing him every day and having his arms around me."

"Then tell him. It's clear that your forgiveness has cleared your head, and you now see him as the man he is. The man you grew to love."

"I can't tell him. It would only complicate things. He's in a relationship, and I can't ruin that. It's not fair. He deserves to be happy."

"You don't think you deserve to be happy?"

"I think I do, but not with him."

"You wanted a friendship with the man you once loved and still love. That can complicate things, and I told you that when you told me the two of you were going to remain friends. There's too much chemistry between the both of you, and your friendship will be a constant struggle."

I didn't reply as the bell went off, and I got up and left his office.

Chapter Thirty-Five

The week went by fast, and I was kept busy between the coffee shop and Sabrina, who kept me on alert for any little change for the party. G and I had gone shopping, and I bought a white, strapless, scalloped-lace, flared, short dress. G practically stopped breathing when I tried it on, and I knew it was the one. Simon hadn't been in the coffee shop all week and I sent him a couple of text messages, but he never replied. He must have been busy with his new girlfriend. I had wondered if he'd bring her to the party. If he did, I didn't know how I would be able to stand it. My eyes started to fill with tears as I stared at myself in the mirror.

"Get him back," G said as she grasped my shoulders.

"It's too late."

"It's never too late for anything you want in life. You've been moping around since Vegas. Whether you want to admit it or not, you're not complete without him."

"Can we please not talk about this right now? You have a very important party coming up tomorrow."

I took in a deep, cleansing breath as I walked through the doors of Simon's house. Sabrina ran over and grabbed my hand, leading me straight into the backyard. I gasped when I saw two swans floating around in the pool. The yard was amazing and so elegant. White tents filled the open areas with white tables and chairs, and the whole yard was lit up like Christmas time with white lights. Flowers, from roses to magnolias, were placed all around, and white candles flickered away.

"Well, what do you think?" Sabrina asked in excitement.

"I think it's elegant, stunning, and the most beautiful thing I've ever seen."

She smiled at me and then took my hand, looking me over from head to toe. "You are stunning. I love that dress. It's what I would have picked for you."

"Thank you. Do you know where Simon is?"

"I think he's upstairs getting dressed. I have to run and make sure the caterers are doing their job. We'll talk later." She kissed me on the cheek.

I walked upstairs, unsure if I should or not, and softly knocked on Simon's bedroom door.

"Simon, it's Gabby."

There was a moment of silence before he told me to come in. When I opened the door, he was sitting on the edge of his bed, putting on his shoes. I sharply inhaled when I saw him in his white suit with a white shirt underneath and the top three buttons undone. He looked like a god, and instantly, my panties were drenched. He stared at me for a brief moment, and I swear I heard a gasp.

"Hello, Gabrielle. You look very beautiful." He got up from the bed and went over to the mirror.

"Hi, Simon. Thank you. You look great. I love the suit."

"Thanks." His smile was soft.

"I sent you a few text messages over the past week, and you never replied."

"Sorry, I've been really busy, and it's been a crazy week."

"I understand. The life of a billionaire running his own company."

"Yeah, something like that. Did you need something?"

My heart ached. I could tell he didn't want me in his room. Maybe his girlfriend was on her way over, and he was afraid she'd come up here and find us.

"I just wanted to tell you that Sabrina did an amazing job with the yard."

"Yes. She did."

Awkward silence set in. "Well, I'm going to head downstairs because G and Donovan should be here any second. I see some guests started to arrive."

"Okay. I'll be down in a minute."

I faked a smile and walked out of the room and down to the bar, where the bartender in white was smiling at me. The same bartender who was at the gala.

"Hey, pretty lady. Whisky sour, double whisky." He smiled.

"That's right. You remembered."

"I never forget a beautiful lady's drink order."

My cheeks heated as he made my drink and handed it to me.

"Gabby! Oh my God. This is…I have no words."

"Isn't it lovely?" I smiled.

"Where's Simon?"

"I'm right here." He smiled as he shook Donovan's hand and gave G a hug.

I had to admit, I could have used a hug from him at this moment. The guests poured in, and the waiters dressed in white walked around with glasses of champagne and appetizers. Simon walked away and went over to talk to some people he knew. Dana walked up to me and grabbed my arm.

"OH MY EFFIN' GOD! I would kill to live in a house like this. I need a rich man in my life. Does he have any rich friends?"

"Why don't you go ask him? He seems to be talking to everyone but me." I walked away and had the bartender make me another whiskey sour.

The air was thick when Simon and I were near each other, and I noticed he made it a point to stay away from me.

"Gabby, I would like you to meet, Justin, my...ahem... friend."

"It's nice to meet you, Justin." I smiled as we lightly hugged.

I looked at Jared. He was beaming from ear to ear. It was a look I once had not too long ago. "Good for you," I mouthed. He gave me a thumbs-up as they walked away.

I happened to glance at the doorway and nearly felt like I was going to pass out when *she* walked in. Simon walked over and gave her a kiss and a hug. *Calm down, Gabby. This is Giana and Donovan's night. Don't ruin it.* My eyes started to tear, so I went inside the house and to the bathroom. When I came out, I saw Simon walk by. He stopped and then looked at me.

"Are you all right?"

"Yeah. Of course. I just had to use the bathroom."

"Your eye looks kind of red."

"I got something in it. Something was in the air

outside. I got it out, and I'm fine now." I walked past him and back to the yard. I needed to make a toast.

I got up on the stage that was built inside the tent and took the microphone from the stand.

"Excuse me, everyone." The tent went silent. "I would like to thank you all for coming here tonight to join in the celebration of two special people, Giana and Donovan."

As I looked out, I saw Simon and her standing next to each other, staring at me. "Giana and I have been best friends/sisters since I was seven years old. She took care of me, and she loved me unconditionally. She was there for me through the good times and the bad. More bad than good, may I add, and I've never been more proud to see her marry the man of her dreams. She has always been an inspiration to me, and no matter where life takes us, we'll always be by each other's side. Here's to you, Giana and Donovan! Curt and Darcy would be so proud!" I winked as I held up my glass. She let out a loud laugh, and then, after everyone cheered, she came up on stage and put her arm around me.

"I love you."

"I love you too."

Everyone sat down at their tables as dinner was being served. My stomach was so twisted that I couldn't eat, so I walked out of the tent and into the house. I stood in the kitchen where the caterers were placing the dishes of food on the trays for the waiters.

"Aren't you going to eat?" a voice behind me spoke.

"No. I'm not hungry." I took a sip of my whiskey sour.

"You need to eat, Gabrielle. You've been drinking."

I was getting angry and unable to control my actions. Why wouldn't he just leave me alone? He sure as hell had no problem doing it ever since I got here. The buildup of everything hit me, and I imploded.

The Secret He Holds

"Why the fuck don't you go back to your girlfriend and leave me the hell alone." I stomped away, but before I could get past him, he grabbed my arm, led me into the library, and slammed the door shut.

"What the fuck are you talking about?"

"You know damn well what I'm talking about. Don't worry. I'll be sure to leave early enough so you can take her upstairs and fuck her."

"You're crazy. You are absolutely nuts. Do you know that?"

"As crazy as they come," I yelled.

He ran his hands through his hair and then took off his jacket.

"You have no idea what you're talking about." He pointed his finger at me in anger.

"Oh, really. I saw the fucking pictures of you and her. She's the reason why you haven't returned any of my text messages and the reason why you felt so guilty for fucking me in Vegas." Tears erupted.

"Seriously, Gabrielle? Are you fucking serious right now? Do you want to know the truth? I felt guilty because you regretted what happened. You, Gabby. Not me. I loved every second of it, and I was so happy to finally think we could make something of ourselves again, but no, you go and tell me it was a mistake, and you blamed it on the alcohol, making me feel like the biggest bastard on the face of this earth. I didn't text you back because I was trying to let you go. I can't do this anymore, Gabrielle. I can't be your friend. I want more. I want you. I want us. A real relationship like we had."

"How can you sit there and tell me that with your girlfriend outside?"

"She's not my girlfriend!" he shouted. "She's my cousin, Marcella. God, Gabrielle, is that what you thought this whole time?" He walked closer to me as one tear escaped my eye.

I nodded my head because I couldn't speak.

He took hold of my hand and gently wiped my tears with his thumb. "She had breast cancer and underwent a double mastectomy when she was thirty. She's thirty-five now, and that was the event we were at. I'm a huge supporter and made a very generous donation."

Oh shit. I felt like an ass now. "I'm sorry. I thought—"

"That explains your behavior. If only you would have asked me about her that night in Vegas. I'm sorry, Gabrielle, and you may not want to hear this, but I am so in love with you. I thought the whole friendship thing could work, but I was wrong. You complete my life, baby. You fill the void that's been inside me all these years. You and nobody else." He softly stroked my face.

I looked up into his beautiful eyes. "I love you too, Simon."

He smiled and leaned closer, brushing his lips over mine. "I want nothing more than to fuck you right here and now, but we better get back to the party before people come looking for us. Tell me you'll spend the night tonight."

"Of course I will. I want nothing more."

He kissed me again and ran his hand up the back of my dress, cupping my ass. "Damn you and that perfect ass."

I laughed as he put his arm around me, and we went back to the party.

"Do you think the swans shit in my pool?"

"Probably." I smiled.

"Great. Just great."

Chapter Thirty-Six

ONE MONTH LATER

We pulled up to Simon's house, and he grabbed the box from the back seat. I saw Greta and Marty in the living room when we walked into the house.

"What's going on here?" I asked as I looked at Simon.

"I figured the house could use a little feng shui."

"Oh my God, really?"

"Yeah. I did some research, and it sounds interesting. Plus, with you moving in, it's your house now, and you should have something that's important to you."

"I already have something that's important to me, and that's all I need." I reached up and kissed his lips.

"I think that box goes up in the bedroom, right?" His smile grew wide.

"I believe it does." I grabbed his hand, he grabbed the box, and we walked upstairs.

~

"I don't understand why I have to wear this blindfold," I said when we were in the back of the limo on our way to the hotel in Barbados.

"I told you it's a surprise. I don't want you to see it until we arrive." He brought my hand up to his lips and kissed it.

"I hate surprises."

"I know you do, but you'll love this one."

The limo stopped, and Simon told me to stay put until he opened the door. I felt his hand on mine as he helped me from the limo.

"Are you ready?"

"Yes." I smiled, wondering what he had up his sleeve.

He took off the blindfold, and we were standing in front of the hotel. I looked up. It was called Gabrielle Mon Amour. I gasped as I put my hand over my mouth and looked at him. As usual, tears sprang to my eyes.

"You named your hotel after me?"

"Yes. Welcome to Gabrielle Mon Amour. Meaning Gabrielle, My Love. I find it quite fitting."

I wrapped my arms around him and hugged him tight, hiding my face in his neck as the tears fell. "I love it so much, and I love you. Thank you," I whispered.

"You're welcome. Now let's go up to our suite. I have another surprise for you."

I wasn't sure my heart could take any more surprises. This was the ultimate gift of love, and I was overjoyed. When he opened the door to the suite, he took my hand and led me to the bedroom. Lying on the bed were two robes; one in black and one in pink. I ran and grabbed the pink one.

"You got the robes."

"Every room has them. Black for men and pink for the ladies."

"Oh, Simon. I'm speechless." I walked over and gave him a long and passionate kiss.

"There's another thing. When we get back from our vacation, Katie will be waiting for you outside your office. She's thrilled to be working for you again."

"What?"

"I need you to come back to Young International. That's where you belong, Gabrielle. Not in a coffee shop. Okay?"

I ran my fingers through his hair as I stared into his eyes. "Okay." I kissed his lips.

We didn't leave the hotel suite the rest of the night.

∽

Six Months Later

I was happier than ever living with Simon and working at Young International. For the first time, my life was complete, and I was right where I belonged. We were sitting in the lounge chairs outside on the patio, sipping mojitos and watching the sunset over the lake.

"I want to marry you, Gabrielle."

I nearly choked on my drink. "What?"

"I'm going to propose to you."

"Oh. Okay."

"Okay?"

"Okay, master?"

He chuckled and then reached in his pocket and pulled out a small box. "I'm serious."

My heart skipped a thousand beats. We had never

talked about marriage except the time he said he didn't believe in it. I gulped as he turned to me.

"I probably should have done this in a more romantic way, but I couldn't wait." He got up from his seat, took my hand, and helped me up. "I love you so much and never want to lose you again. You've turned my entire world upside down, and I like it. You are the most beautiful and intelligent woman I have ever laid eyes on, and you mean more to me than anything else in my life. Words can't even describe my love for you, baby. So, will you please do me the honor of becoming my wife and spending the rest of your life with me? If you say yes, I'll give you the world. Well, I'll still give you the world, even if you say no." He smiled as he slipped the enormous diamond on my finger.

"Yes, I will marry you, Simon," I squealed as I threw my arms around his neck. "I love you so much, and I want nothing more than to spend the rest of my life with you."

"You have no idea how happy I am to hear that." He picked me up and carried me up to our bedroom.

Finally, I had the one thing I'd searched for my entire life—a love that was beyond measure and someone who loved me more than life itself. I was living my dream life thanks to a man named Simon Young.

Thank you for reading The Secret He Holds. I hope you enjoyed it.

Be sure to check out "More Sizzling Romance for more of my romance reads!

I invite you to join my Sandi's Romance Readers Facebook Group, where we talk about books, romance, and more! Join the fun!

Newsletter
Website
Facebook
Instagram
FOLLOW ME ON AMAZON
TikTok
Bookbub
Goodreads

More Sizzling Romance

Looking for more romance reads about billionaires, second chances, and sports? Check out my other romance novels and escape to another world and from the daily grind of life – one book at a time.

Series:

Forever Series
Forever Black (Forever, Book 1)
Forever You (Forever, Book 2)
Forever Us (Forever, Book 3)
Being Julia (Forever, Book 4)
Collin (Forever, Book 5)
A Forever Family (Forever, Book 6)
A Forever Christmas (Holiday short story)

Wyatt Brothers
Love, Lust & A Millionaire (Wyatt Brothers, Book 1)
Love, Lust & Liam (Wyatt Brothers, Book 2)

More Sizzling Romance

A Millionaire's Love
Lie Next to Me (A Millionaire's Love, Book 1)
When I Lie with You (A Millionaire's Love, Book 2)

Happened Series
Then You Happened (Happened Series, Book 1)
Then We Happened (Happened Series, Book 2)

Redemption Series
Carter Grayson (Redemption Series, Book 1)
Chase Calloway (Redemption Series, Book 2)
Jamieson Finn (Redemption Series, Book 3)
Damien Prescott (Redemption Series, Book 4)

Interview Series
The Interview: New York & Los Angeles Part 1
The Interview: New York & Los Angeles Part 2

Love Series:
Love In Between (Love Series, Book 1)
The Upside of Love (Love Series, Book 2)

Wolfe Brothers
Elijah Wolfe (Wolfe Brothers, Book 1)
Nathan Wolfe (Wolfe Brothers, Book 2)
Mason Wolfe (Wolfe Brothers, Book 3)

Kind Brothers
One of a Kind (Kind Brothers Series, Book 1)
Two of a Kind (Kind Brothers Series, Book 2)
Three of a Kind (Kind Brothers Series, Book 3)
Four of a Kind (Kind Brothers Series, Book 4)
Five of a Kind (Kind Brothers Series, Book 5)
The Kind Brothers (Kind Brothers Series, Book 6)

More Sizzling Romance

Six of a Kind (Kind Brothers Series, Book 7)
Seven of a Kind (Kind Brothers Series, Book 8)
Eight of a Kind (Kind Brothers Series, Book 9)
Nine of a Kind (Kind Brothers Series, Book 10)
A Kind Wedding: Jackson & Georgia (Kind Brothers Series, Book 11)
A Kind Wedding: Conner & Charlotte (Kind Brothers Series, Book 12)
A Kind Wedding: Nathan & Sofia (Kind Brothers Series, Book 13)
A Kind Wedding: Christian & Charleigh (Kind Brothers Series, Book 14)
Ten of a Kind (Kind Brothers Series, Book 15)
Eleven of a Kind (Kind Brothers Series, Book 16)
Twelve of a Kind (Kind Brothers Series, Book 17)

Standalone Books
The Billionaire's Christmas Baby
His Proposed Deal
The Secret He Holds
The Seduction of Alex Parker
Something About Lorelei
One Night in London
The Exception
Corporate Assets
A Beautiful Sight
The Negotiation
Defense
The Con Artist
#Delete
Behind His Lies
One Night in Paris
Perfectly You
The Escort

More Sizzling Romance

The Ring
The Donor
Rewind
Remembering You
When I'm With You
LOGAN (A Hockey Romance)
The Merger
Baby Drama
Unspoken
The Property Brokers

Printed in Great Britain
by Amazon